Best Wishes,

# And While My Body Sleeps

# And While My Body Sleeps

## ADRIENNE FELICE

Rutledge Books, Inc.  Danbury, CT

Interior design by Al Robinson

Cover design by Elizabeth Mihaltse

Copyright © 2001 by Adrienne Felice

ALL RIGHTS RESERVED
Rutledge Books, Inc.
107 Mill Plain Road, Danbury, CT 06811
1-800-278-8533
www.rutledgebooks.com

Manufactured in the United States of America

**Cataloging in Publication Data**
Felice, Adrienne
    And While My Body Sleeps

    ISBN: 1-58244-142-1

    1. Fiction

Library of Congress Control Number: 2001088144

# Dedication

This book is dedicated to my mother, Grace Marie, who taught me to see the beauty and the art in the written word. To my grandmother, Margaret, who continues, even from spirit to bolster me with her strength of character. To the many fine teachers who have taught me to approach life through the constancy of spirituality. This book, a gift, is a tribute to all of you. And in turn, I present it to all that will take advantage of its lessons, as I have. May God bless us all.

# *Introduction*

·····································

This book has been written with gratitude for the lessons of which I chose to take advantage. Lessons which, applied when I was at the lowest point in my life, rescued me from what seemed an interminable state of depression and lack of control.

I know I relate, to many readers, with the type of suffering one endures when labeled with depression.

But whether suffering from depression or not, these lessons are important to us all. The first and most important lesson, that you have control. The second, learning of your true nature-you create and draw your own environment, good or bad. The third, learning to see existence as it truly is. How to conduct your life as the symphony it was meant to be. How to learn the lessons you set out to learn and then move on. How to heal from what seems incurable. How to live your life for the joy of it and see the endless beauty that is eternity of which you are an important and irreplaceable soul.

Through the magic of storytelling, I have written many of my own experiences and some of the experiences of others, in order to teach and bring the reader back to what he/she already knows on a subliminal level. Where we came from, where we are going, who we are, and just how loved and important, unique and irreplaceable each of us is. No matter our past, no matter our lessons as we perceive them, accomplished or failed.

As you sit with this book, my wish for you, when all reading is done is that it will be only the beginning in your search for self and your place in the vast universe of existence. Finding our path is an easy task when we step out of our own way. May you find that strength as I have and may you see the joy and beauty that was always there waiting simply for your recognition. If this writing is able to escort you through that door, then it has accomplished its goal. As the Professor will tell you in the following pages, not one of us will be left behind. Each of us is an essential piece of art in the gallery that is eternity.

Take this journey at your own pace, in your own time. It is one you will never regret taking.

At the age of four, what seemed to be my predilection for depression began with some unfortunate events in my life. This shadow would follow me for the next twenty-eight years when I was finally diagnosed with severe clinical depression. Raised to be suspicious of the least of medications, I refused the brain-altering drugs that were offered to me. However, I realized that I could not continue my life under this intolerable mental restriction.

Oddly, also from an early age, I had many experiences people would refer to as psychic or unexplainable. This bolstered my spirituality and peaked my curiosity about such things. It seemed, throughout this difficult time, I was, nevertheless, drawn to teachers who could teach me about the spiritual disciplines. However, trying to apply them to my life, which was sickened with depression, they seemed only to be lovely, unob-tainable dreams-beautiful rhetoric, which could only give me temporary relief in a growing imprisonment that was depression.

At the time of my diagnosis, I decided to attempt meditation as an alternative to medication, although I did not know that people used meditation to alleviate depression. I simply knew that drugs were not an answer for me and that I had to find a different way.

I chose Transcendental Meditation and began the journey that saved my life. My teacher, bless her, was and is a patient and understanding person and a tribute to the method she teaches. When she taught me the technique, she told me it was as though I "fell" into it. The truth is I was so desperate that I plunged myself into it! In her company, the meditation went smoothly and was very relaxing. Little did I know that her own energy made it so and that I was in for the roller coaster ride of my life!

For the next week, when I would sit down to meditate as instructed, tears would seem to flow out of nowhere, and I felt more out of control than ever. I would call her on the phone and tell her what a terrible time I was having. Apparently I was look-ing for some instant cure that would take me into an alternate reality, fix me and drop me back into the world. It didn't work that way.

"Andrea," I would say, "I can't do this anymore!" She would calmly reply, "Those are the good ones, Adrienne. Go do some more!"

After a week of this, the tears finally stopped and the medita-tion became relaxing and comforting. I used it as an escape from the torment of the day. I would tell myself that my meditation would make me feel better and look forward to the two twenty minute sessions.

After six months, I like to tell people that I discovered flowers for the first time in my life! As though they had been hidden from me, here were these beautiful creations that I had never really seen before.

One of the difficulties of depression, for me, was a terrible fear of people. I found it so difficult to talk to anyone as though they were waiting for me to say the wrong thing so they could bring out a menacing ax and annihilate me! It seems that through mediation we find subtle ways to repair the problems we create. My fear of people was alleviated when I began to see a strange warm light in the eyes of friends, family and even strangers.

Instinctively I began to realize that what I was looking at was the light of the human soul. A light I began to see in my own eyes. There was a connection. We were the same. We were made of the same stuff, regardless of our background, the color of our skin, the years of or lack of education. We were all the same. I would have to fear myself if I were to continue fearing others. Consequently, the fear softened and melted, replaced over the years by understanding and love. This, finally, is a comfortable life.

And now, my book. I had been told, even through the worst years of my illness, that I came to this world to teach-that I would find the method in my own time, in my own way.

"Funny, " I would think, "I couldn't help myself, how would I teach others?" Well, here it is: the book that teaches all that I have learned, the hard way, through experience, pain, hardship and finally joy. It is possible. Everything is possible with the determination of the god force in each of us, the human spirit, the human soul.

And now, my friends, your journey begins. . .

# Prologue

............................

Certainly we take life for granted. Of course, we know its progression. Surely, it will respond in kind, as that of our parents, our grandparents, etc. But will it? How much seems in our control? Not as much as we would hope. Underlying fear of a society gone mad paints images we cannot bear to face. And those who depend on us, those whose very lives were entrusted to our care, we tell them no harm will come to them because we are there. We tell them that they are the most important part of our lives, that without them we ourselves would cease to exist. But in this world of uncommunicated values that laughs at constraint, manners, authority, in our "feel good at all cost" society; how do we protect our children until they are capable of protecting themselves? How indeed.

Nothing in this world could be as frightening as losing a child. Can one feel more helpless, more out of control, than to care for a child, one who has stolen one's heart since its cataclysmic inception into this world, who then, without warning, is simply taken from one's life? It is hard to imagine the feelings of inadequacy when an innocent who trusts is stolen from one's environment, an innocent who believes in the absolute love and unconditional protection of parents. Can we alter these events? Can we protect our children?

Annette is such a child. Four years old, she is blonde and precocious. She is an only child and for that reason has had attention lavished on her from her two adoring parents. She is intelligent beyond her years. She is secure in the knowledge that she is loved and cared for. And now she is gone. Simply gone. For two days this little girl has been missing. For two days her frantic parents have not slept. Two long, agonizing days, they have taken turns looking for her and keeping a vigil by the phone. Dear, sweet Annette. What has happened to this little girl?

"Joseph, I'm on the phone with the police. Hello, Sergeant Schaefer, this is Mrs. Lawrence. I've heard nothing about my daughter, Sergeant."

"Mrs. Lawrence, we know nothing, but we're working on it. Believe me, when we have some information, anything, I will call."

"Annette is a little girl, Sergeant, she's only four. It's been two days!" The hysteria in her voice mounting, Mrs. Lawrence tried to contain herself and go on. "What can I do? I can't just sit here by the phone. Please, she's my little girl, please!" With that Mrs. Lawrence lost what little self-control she had left and slumped in tears.

"Hello, Sergeant, this is Joe."

"I am so sorry, Mr. Lawrence. I wish I could help. I know the waiting is agony. I have kids of my own, you know. I promise, we are doing everything possible."

"How does a child disappear from her own backyard in broad daylight? She was only alone for a minute!"

"Try not to blame yourself, Mr. Lawrence; it happens every day. I wish I could say it was unusual, but it isn't. These people are good at what they do and kids are too trusting."

Sergeant Schaefer was a good man. If he had any faults at all, then caring too much would have been one of them. His heart went out to the Lawrence family. And thoughts of Annette, lost, hurt, or worse kept him worrying as he worked to find her. A four-year-old child, alone in an all too often unfeeling world. It was too much to think about. He had to stay in control for Annette's sake. Somehow they had to find her. His thoughts momentarily drifted to his own children. They were grown now, but his career had shown him just how horrible this world could be for children. He was fortunate that nothing devastating had ever happened in his own family. But what if it had? What would he have done? He shook off the depressed intense anxiety that thought presented to him. Where in the world was Annette?

"Sergeant Schaefer, you have a call on line two. It's the Chicago police about a missing girl."

"Mr. Lawrence, I have to put you on hold. Don't hang up. I'll take this call and only be a minute. Hello, this is Sergeant Schaefer."

"Sergeant Schaefer, this is Captain McClinton with the Chicago PD. We have a female child here. She says her name is Annette. She is approximately four years old, blonde, blue eyes and she fits the missing person description we received over the wire. She's wearing blue jeans and a pink sweater."

"Is she all right, Captain?"

"She's just fine. She has quite an imagination, this little one. She's been keeping us entertained with stories of angels!"

"Put her on the phone, Captain. Annette, this is Sergeant Schaefer. Annette, what is your dolly's name?"

"Gloria, do you know her?" a timid bewildered innocent voice hesitantly spoke.

"I sure do, Sweetheart! I am going to make sure you and Gloria and Mommy and Daddy are all together very soon. Let me talk to the policeman again. Captain McClinton, that's her! How did you find her?"

"I wish I could tell you we did. Actually, she found us. She walked right up to a beat cop on State Street and told him the angels said he would help her go home. We got lucky with this one, Sergeant."

"We sure did. Thank God! Hell, thank the angels!" Sergeant Schaefer could not contain his excitement. Delighted, he switched lines back to Mr. Lawrence.

"Hello, Mr. Lawrence? She's all right. She's safe. She's at the police station in Chicago, but she's all right."

They laughed, they cried, and they made plans.

Sergeant Schaefer had done the inadvisable in this case; he had gotten personally involved.

"I'll pick you up in my squad car. We'll drive to Chicago and pick her up. Oh, and bring Gloria."

The three of them drove together to Chicago to bring Annette home. It was a two-hour drive from the small town in Indiana, but it was the happiest trip any of them could remember taking. They chatted as though they had known each other for a lifetime. It is interesting how near tragedy can bring out brotherly feelings in perfect strangers. How we depend on each other in times of crisis, not seeing differences anymore, not standing on protocol, not heeding lack of familiarity, just meeting needs. Having barely pulled to the curb in front of their destination, Mrs. Lawrence fairly flew out of the vehicle and into the building, followed closely by her husband and Sergeant Schaefer.

"Baby, are you all right?"

"Mommy!" A reunion. A family united with a happy ending for a change. Sergeant Schaefer looked on wishing they could all end like this.

Captain McClinton joined Sergeant Schaefer. They both felt out of place observing what certainly was a private family moment.

Captain McClinton absolved these feelings by turning his attention to Sergeant Schaefer and filling him in on theories of this and similar cases.

"We think the abductor is part of a group selling small children, a kind of white slavery operation. They export them to Middle Eastern countries where towheads like Annette are in great demand. We've been working on this for quite a while. If it's as big as we think it is, they're in practically every state. The women who entice these kids away from their homes are the elderly grandmother type. They've really thought this one through. Everybody trusts someone who looks like their grandmother. Annette said she offered to bake her cookies, take her shopping, and buy her ice cream.

The only thing we can't figure out is this angel stuff. The kid insists some angels helped her get out of the room she was kept in and stayed with her until she saw a policeman. Then they told her to run to him and that they would watch her until they knew she was safe. At first, I thought some vigilante group was working on this case with us, but it was all her little fantasy. Someone there must have tripped up and left the door unlocked. I figure Annette was so scared that she started hallucinating; but we can't shake her story. Anyway, what does it matter; at least we got one back."

"Honest, Mommy, the angels helped me get out of that room. They got the door open."

"How many angels were there, Sweetheart?"

"A bunch!"

"Did they have wings?"

"I didn't see their wings, Mommy; but they must have. They were angels! They took me for a walk until we found the big policeman. Then they told me to run to him and ask him to help me. And he did! The angels said they would help me find you. The angels said they would help me go home."

# Chapter 1

Why on Earth would Meredith want to move to Wisconsin? Calvert, I never heard of this place. What is this woman up to now?

Anyone with friends like Meredith Tolworth is a stranger to boredom. But friend she is. One I could not imagine being without. Somehow, she has managed to train me, like Pavlov's dog, to relate her voice to new adventure; always life changing; always involving growth . . . usually mine.

Do I seem the type who would have a psychic New Age counselor for a pal? Hardly. Although parapsychology is my department at Hardwick University, I am a scientist. Well, I was trained as one, anyway. And believe me, I look the part. Early forties, my wardrobe consists of grey suits and lab coats. Since the inception of this department some ten years ago, my wardrobe has stayed the same, but my psyche grew.

Meredith was one of those unexpected benefits that

came with my department. Were I asked to describe her, I would use terms such as lithe, tall, and ageless. She is my age, but you would be at a loss to guess it. She keeps her polished hair at shoulder length. It's dark and glossy like a mirror.

There is an air of mystery surrounding Meredith. Until you get to know her down-to-earth, matter-of-fact way of dealing with people, she would impress you as aristocratic and worldly. Had she been at a loss for a career, the modeling world would have accepted her with open arms. But from the time she was a small child, she was driven by a world few of us see. Her curiosity about what I teach brought her to me. But I realized, in this world of the paranormal, I was the novice caught in a rut of scientific data, and trying to sort that from experience. Meredith, in a sense, became my teacher.

"Langston Paul Evans - Professor of Parapsychology" is the sign that sits on my desk. But Meredith, due to her unfaltering wisdom, has helped me to grow in a world I always knew existed, but one in which I had little background. Not in this lifetime, anyway. Talents seemed to have followed me from somewhere. Abilities, which were apparently mine, caught me within the dichotomy of knowing truth and experiencing the current world I was born to and the realities carefully taught to me. Effecting the transition of allowing what I knew to be real to flow through me naturally was Meredith's contribution to my life.

Although I tried to approach my career from a completely scientific perspective, I have crossed thresholds timidly, but surely. Certainly never to return again. All of this with the help of my dearest friend.

And what has become of my dear friend Meredith? With no warning, no preparation, this willful mysterious woman has packed and is planning a move from Virginia to Wisconsin. Why, in heaven's name? That is a question for which I intend to have an answer.

"Meredith, I heard your message on my answering machine. What are you up to? You left on vacation two weeks ago, and now you're moving? And Wisconsin of all places; do you know what kind of winter you are in for? What on Earth possessed you? Is there some sort of trouble? I thought you liked Virginia. You never spoke of moving before."

"Well, Lang, if you'd let me get a word in, I'll explain. Actually, I would prefer to explain in person."

"You're coming home?"

"No, Dear Heart, you're coming here."

"What? Have you lost your mind? Classes start in less than a month. I can't be chasing you halfway across the continent. Come home! Stop this nonsense now!"

"I know you must think I have taken leave of my senses, Lang. Please, if you've ever had any faith in our friendship, pack a bag. Your ticket is waiting at the airport. We will meet you on this end."

"We? Who the devil is WE?"

"Lang, hurry, your plane leaves in two hours. Just go!"

Well, that's Meredith. If I argue when she's this determined, I will only find out why I shouldn't have. And yes, I admit to having faith in this friendship.

Meredith had become more than a friend. She had become family. Family, or the accepted description, had eluded me most of my life. I grew up in a stable, sterilized world, abundant in education and material gain; but void of passionate commitment. As a product of this world, I kept to myself.

Finding interest only in my work, I studied psychology, playing down the extra sensory gifts I apparently was born with. They invoked emotions, almost drawing off of them, and that was not part of my upbringing. But I could not have ignored my own destiny any more than I could have gone through life with my eyes sewn shut. As I realized parapsychology was my future, I confronted parents who were less than amused with my revelation. They emphatically discouraged my calling and they had nearly won. After all, in their chosen field of medicine, there was no room for psychic chicanery. The paranormal was a poor attempt at calling attention to one's self. It had no merit, no purpose or meaning. It could not be studied, dissected, or otherwise observed. Surely, it was based on illusion and trickery. A magic show at best. A method to confuse and control the masses at worst. I had been born to two parents who devoted their lives to their scientific professions. Nothing more. They were doctors, and my fantasies about a world they could not see were an embarrassing disgrace to be discouraged. They chided me into reanalyzing my goals. They, after all, were known in their community for straightforward practical medicine and medical research. I was, when all was said and done, an embarrassment. How could I not follow the path they had so cautiously led me on? But how could I not follow my heart and what I knew to be truth? And so, as I strayed from the "norm," my family, realizing I was not one of them, quietly and without ceremony, went about their business and left me to mine. I guess I had always felt alone in this world. I was different. I had abilities not applauded in the Evans' circles.

And just when I had given up hope of finding a kindred spirit, miraculously, Meredith appeared. Meredith should well have been my family. Our backgrounds of early psychic experiences were strikingly similar. The only real difference being that Meredith was encouraged to hone and enhance her psychic abilities. Her parents were as psychically gifted as she was.

As a psychic, she left me in the dust. As a scientist, I was her mentor. It seemed a union drawn by fate. And so I asked myself, did I trust this woman who spent so many years affirming and applauding my research and my personal spiritual growth? Could she get me on a plane on a moment's notice with little or no explanation but that it was important I join her? Without question. I was on my way to Calvert, Wisconsin.

True to her word, my ticket was waiting at the airport. I boarded the plane with moments to spare. Some nagging impression told me I was doing the right thing, that this was important. But aside from intuition and feelings, I had no way of telling what the future was about to produce. It didn't matter. I felt I needed a change. At this moment, any change would do. I was heartsick and ready to cast my fate to the wind. My carefully planned future was falling down around me.

That summer had been less than a success. My career at Hardwick seemed to be plummeting. My department was no longer in my control. Hardwick was experiencing financial difficulty and my department was being cut to the bone. Everything I wanted to add or change became the current topic for argument.

Few things were accepted, the most important of which was denied. I had felt that true students of this art/science needed a foundation on which to build what they would learn and experience. I did not want them to leave my class with only the thought of possibility in the psychic realm. I wanted them to leave with experience. My students would know more than what percentage of right answers showed a possible extra sensory ability in a guessing game. They would know a world beyond the one they lived in.

They would see, as I see, true reality. I knew that in order to understand the world my students were being introduced to, they must become meditators. They had to learn how to transcend from their accepted reality and delve into the myriad of experience and expression in this universe. I chose the medium I was most accustomed to and proceeded to involve a fine teacher. Today I discovered the project was cut. No discussion, no compromise; funds would not allow another addition to faculty. I had become disillusioned. I knew I could not teach effectively with these restrictions.

Time flew by in this world between worlds. Lights instructing passengers to fasten seatbelts caught my attention and pulled me out of my dilemma. Somewhere below us, below clouds that blocked our vision, was Calvert.

The plane made its descent, accompanied by shimmering rays from a brilliant August sun. Nature could calm my nerves with nothing more than the spectacle of her dazzling beauty. Nature assured me of the vastness of her power, and the limited scope of my problems. This, too, would pass. If nothing else, maybe this little trip would help to clear my head.

We descended on what took shape as an innocent, understated rural town. A small, peaceful setting already hinting of upcoming fall colors. The air was fresh and clean as I walked out the front door of the terminal.

A full-length Cadillac limousine sat gloriously at the curb. Peaking out the window, smiling as usual, was my dear friend Meredith. Smiling. She was probably secretly hysterical at the thought of getting me on a plane on a moment's notice to fly to God knows where for God knows what. Noticing that glint in her eye, I felt I really needed to re-evaluate the amount of control this woman had over me. Nevertheless, I was delighted to see her.

"Lang, I want you to meet Gabrielle Lambeau."

A petite, auburn-haired young woman smiled at me as I climbed in the limo and politely extended her hand. As this vast machine rolled elegantly away from the curb, she began to tell me of Calvert, anxious to point out all its advantages. I heard her words, but more importantly, I surveyed an aura. Lovely blue in color, but tinged in brown and shattered as a view through broken glass. Such a young beautiful woman to be experiencing such pain. And from what, I wondered?

My reverie broken by the insistence of her sweet light voice, I listened as she described this place. She was quite proud of Calvert, and for some unknown reason, it seemed important to her that I saw it as she did. She described, in detail, all of Calvert's attributes, its people and the type of lifestyle I could expect to encounter.

"I hope you will like Calvert, Professor Evans. It's a small town, but it's quite picturesque. We have cultural events on a regular basis and we encourage art and museum pieces to be displayed whenever possible. The people here are very charming. I am certain you will find yourself in your element."

I had to be impressed with the enthusiasm contained in this speech. What in heaven's name was this all about? I surveyed Meredith's expression with curiosity, but my intuition was dormant. I hadn't a clue. And this young woman's shattered aura had disturbed me. Possibly all of this had something to do with Ms. Lambeau. Foolishness, surely Meredith would not drop her entire life and run to save a total stranger. Well, knowing Meredith, yes she would. Once again, I turned my attention to the scenery moving past us. We were moving through what looked like the background for a movie, something designed by Rockwell himself. Lovely rolling landscapes, planted to perfection with the elegance of trees seeing centuries of life, and flower and foliage playfully coloring their bountiful environment, lending framework to charming substantial homes.

"It's an impressive setting, Ms. Lambeau."

"Bree, please, Professor Evans."

"Lang, please, Bree."

We laughed lightheartedly at these Victorian manners.

Victorian, yes, that was what she was. A Victorian woman caught in the wrong century.

Somehow, Bree seemed to invoke the charming protective instinct of the Victorian-bred male.

Regardless, she had won me over. I was enraptured, but still in the dark. And apparently I was to remain there for a while.

"I must say I might like it better if I knew why I was summoned here."

"Summoned is a good word, Lang. Destiny is an even better word." Meredith looked at me in the coquettish way she had about her when she knew she was privy to information I had yet to learn. She seemed to glean great delight in confusing the teacher and availed herself of every possible opportunity to indulge in this pastime. Ours was a relationship that kept me on my toes.

"Meredith, I hope you have a very good reason for all of this. Otherwise, I may have a hand in your destiny." I winked at her playfully, but noticed Bree's obvious discomfort with our conversation, sensing incorrectly that I was unhappy with my present predicament. "Don't worry, Bree. We banter back and forth like this all the time. We really are great friends."

With that reassurance, Bree's expression brightened and she seemed to open up again.

"I have been so excited about meeting you for the first time. You know, Meredith and I have discussed this possibility for months."

"Months?" I flashed a look at Meredith which could have melted stone. "Something you may have forgotten to mention, Meredith?"

Bree continued her welcome speech without noticing my look of agitated amusement. As much as I love Meredith, she can be exasperating.

"We have just turned into my driveway, Lang. We will be

home in minutes. I have requested a late supper. We can talk, eat, and relax, my three favorite pastimes."

The driveway ribboned ahead, guided by tall ardent pine trees. Finally, in the distance I saw a house that could easily have held the entire student body at Hardwick. It loomed ahead of us like something out of a Dickens' classic. Majestic and Victorian, just as I expected. It was appropriate for this delicate, anachronistic Victorian maiden. Three stories tall, a brick fortress complete with turret and extended veranda. We walked in the door only to step back in time. The decor in the house was lavish and complimentary to the architectural style in which it was built. From the damask drapes to the embossed leather handpainted wallpaper, this home was trapped in some sort of time warp. And yet, somehow, it all seemed to work. Its mistress was radiant in this setting. She was in her element. Her aura seemed less fragmented here. Obviously, being home alleviated some of her anxiety, but not all. It was a puzzle. One so young who seemed to have everything what could have devastated her so?

"Max will show you to your room and have your luggage brought up. You might want to freshen up and rest before dinner. I have requested it to be served at eight, if this is all right with both of you. The dining room is off the great hall to the left of the staircase. I will see you both then. I am so happy both of you are here. I feel this is the beginning of a wonderful friendship. Somehow, adventure seems imminent. Don't you feel it?"

I had succumbed to an unexpected feeling of comfort in this house, wondering when I would awaken from this dream. The decor, the company, I couldn't have imagined a more comfortable and charming setting. I was beginning to feel as though I belonged here, a sense of homecoming I couldn't explain.

"Follow me, please." Max led the way to the upstairs guest

room. Green. I have always been comfortable in green surroundings. Sometimes I engulf myself in green during meditation. It seems to relax me and yet not interfere with those creative impulses I have come to rely on through the years. This room was as exquisite as the rest of the house. Feminine Victorian charm permeated the green silk wallpaper and matching drapes. The furniture was solid mahogany and heavily carved, an antique dealer's dream. After settling in I realized I hadn't meditated. The fresh crisp air was an added benefit to meditation and I lazily enjoyed the endorfinated state, not realizing the quick passage of time.

"Lang, dinner." Meredith's unmistakable voice broke my reverie. "Bree is waiting for us downstairs. You look rested."

"I must admit, something about this place suits me."

"I knew it would."

"Meredith, how long have you been plotting this?" The impish grin on her face was one of victory. Once more I had been outwitted by my illustrious companion. But to what end?

"Our destinies are intertwined, Lang. Yours, Bree's, and mine; we couldn't escape if we tried. It's too important. You will see; this is all for the best."

The dining room was set with candles, crystal, and fine china. A magnificent crystal chandelier illuminated the room and a gilded mirror, angled to reflect the table setting, took on a life of its own with the help of the twinkling candlelight.

"I am vegetarian, Lang, I hope that's all right with you."

"Bree, that makes three of us. Please, tell me about the history of this chandelier. Certainly it's not a new acquisition."

Bree looked lovingly at the chandelier as if she were introducing an old friend. "This is one of my favorite pieces in the house. It was here when my father bought the house for my mother as a wedding gift. It had not been used since the turn of the century, and had to be modified to be put back into use. The saga of the chandelier was my favorite family story on Christmas morning. My parents would laugh recalling the frustration of disassembling this great monstrosity for an electrician to take it from the house and update it to be used again."

"So it was operated with gas at one time."

"Only partially. At the turn of the century, electricity was already installed in some homes; however, most thought it was a passing fad. Consequently, the chandelier had some electric lights and the rest were operated with gas."

The chandelier twinkled merrily as if it were applauding the story of its life. I could imagine this delightful conversation on Christmas morning.

Bree's knowledge of the late nineteenth century showed a loving interest. I wondered if she was aware of her existence during that period. I also had a strong impression of her longing to return to it on a subliminal level.

"My compliments to your cook, Bree."

"It wasn't easy to find one whose expertise was vegetarian cooking, but I finally came across Anne. More tea, Lang?"

"Yes, thank you. Now, ladies, I have been kept in the dark long enough. Please fill me in on these plans I seem to be part of."

Bree laughed nervously. She made a charming picture of a hostess holding an antique china teapot. "Meredith, would you care to take the floor?"

"No, Bree, I'm in over my head already. I swept this poor man off on a plane on a moment's notice. Please, I think you might be better suited to the job."

"Certainly one of you could muster enough courage to speak."

"Of course, Lang, I would be happy to." Bree smiled. "You see, I have been interested in the occult for years. My parents died in an auto crash in France ten years ago while I was in boarding school."

That was it. That broken heart and the look of despondency that went with it. It was a loss that manifested itself in her aura. That was the part of Bree that had not yet healed. "Of course. I knew something had devastated you."

Meredith intercepted a growing look of confusion on Bree's face. "He's apparently read your aura, Bree. It's all right. You will get used to the casual way Professor Evans uses his abilities." Meredith smiled in my direction. She knew I could be abrupt. She also knew it was unintentional.

"Please, Bree; I did not mean to alarm you. Meredith is right. You have a lovely color to your aura, but it's broken and tinged in brown, an unmistakable sadness seems to permeate it, as though something had affected you so adversely you have had trouble recovering from it."

"My parents' deaths came as quite a shock, Lang; and you are right, I have never really recovered from the experience. I have wondered about their fate. Where are they? Are they together? Are they happy? I have been unable to answer these questions to my satisfaction. I have no natural psychic ability as you. I was raised in the Catholic religion and admonished about such things. But my religion has been no comfort to me as I have tried to cope with my loss. It has answered none of my questions. I have been told that I must accept comfort through my faith; and I have tried. Surely, the priests have meant well, but my faith has been shaken after losing my parents so early in life. My religion, as well meaning as it is, has not helped me with my greatest need. On a trip east, I audited one of your lectures, and met Meredith at the same time. I was impressed with not only your knowledge, but your enthusiasm. You spoke of spiritual awareness during that lecture and it seemed as though you were not only teaching, but leading.

Showing the way, so to speak, as if you had answered my prayers. I needed someone of your intelligence and background to maintain what I had so desperately hoped would be the truth; that there is life after death. Meredith was so kind that day. We met just as the lecture was starting, and afterward went out for coffee. I filled her in on my mission, a sort of female Houdini out to prove life after death. I, of course, hope that I will meet with more success than he did."

Ever the teacher, I am driven to perpetuate correct information at all costs: "Actually, Bree, there is reason to believe that Houdini may have met with complete success in proving life after death. A book written by the great Spiritualist Minister, Arthur Ford, reveals the rather lengthy message Ford delivered to Houdini's wife proving to her satisfaction that Houdini had indeed survived death. It spelled out: 'Rosabelle, believe.' It was written in code and quite complicated, invoking preplanned responses in order that it not be easily guessed. Arthur Ford was a talented psychic and having studied much of his work, I am inclined to accept the accuracy of his documentation that this message was delivered as planned."

Bree looked a bit puzzled. "If that is the truth, why isn't it recognized by the Houdini museum in Appleton? Surely, proving life after death is no piece of useless information."

"You wouldn't think so, but you have to remember that the entire time period was mesmerized and romanticized by the growing popularity of Spiritualism. This religion was founded just seven years before the turn of the twentieth century and gained immense popularity. It became quite fashionable. As with most popular things the temptation to turn it into a money-making scheme, for some, was impossible to resist. This wore away its credibility as well as the credibility of its practitioners. As Houdini proved to the world, there were far too many fakes making easy money preying off of the wretched emotions of those who had lost loved ones. This did nothing for those who, like Arthur Ford, were legitimate. And yet, Houdini believed enough to continue his search, even after his own death. Although Spiritualism claims its basis in Christianity, some Christian religions saw it as direct opposition to their own doctrine. The truth, I am afraid, is buried in beliefs and opinions. But, as with many 'facts' in the psychic realm, it is personal experience and growth that really counts. This type of growth, discouraged by your church, is encouraged and necessary in psychic awareness. We will never ask you to accept anything on faith alone. We will encourage you to develop your awareness and experience for yourself."

Bree seemed to brighten at this prospect. "That is what I want, Lang, first-hand experience, so that no one can tell me what to believe or how I should feel. But I have to admit feelings of hesitation and some fear. I guess being told to avoid such things is engraved in my subconscious. How could one communicate with the dead, Lang? I mean, if one really wanted to?"

"And you really do want to, don't you, Bree? That would certainly secure at least the beginning of a personal healing for you. The fear you speak of is a normal reaction to something you have been taught should be avoided. But fear is something you will have to overcome in order to progress in the direction you are choosing."

Bree's wide-eyed look of innocence and wonder was certainly compelling. Meredith smiled in silent agreement.

"Bree, you communicate without even knowing it. The only thing that keeps you from being consciously aware of such communication is the fear you speak of."

"I am afraid I don't understand."

"Meredith, you've been silent too long. We could use one of your anecdotes."

"You walk into a dark room, Bree. You reach for a light switch. As your hand touches the light switch, and before you can turn on the light, someone unknown to you grabs your hand. How would you react?"

"I think I would have a heart attack!"

"Exactly. Now, you walk into a dark room, switch on the light, and Uncle John comes in and takes your hand. No heart attack, right?"

"Well, yes. Of course, I see what you mean."

"The human brain is designed to protect its own sanity and housing above all else. When confronted with something we are not familiar with, such as psychic awareness, we often just block it out. The fear might be too much for us. And, all too often, in most of our Christian religions, we have been warned against furthering our awareness. So, essentially, we ignore everything outside of our own physical environment. It's as though we have chosen to live in a shadow box, and refuse to see there is life outside of it! For example, are you familiar with psychokinesis?"

"I've read something about it. Is it moving objects through thought?"

"That's right, Bree. The way it is taught proves my point. A student of psychokinesis starts by trying to move a toothpick around in a glass of water. Now, if you saw a toothpick moving through water, that wouldn't frighten you too much, would it?"

"No, of course not."

"This exercise slowly and gently introduces psychokinesis to the brain. Then gradually, after mastering this, the student moves on to bigger things. The ability has been established, and the fear diminished."

Meredith could certainly paint a verbal picture. I'd come to rely on these little narratives to easily teach an otherwise difficult concept.

"Well put, Meredith. Then, Bree, the task becomes to alleviate the fear, open yourself up to possibility and, ultimately, experience greater and greater awareness within your own reality. The seemingly magic key to all of this is meditation. Just recognizing the possibility brings the reality of psychic phenomena into your world; but meditation conditions the reflex, causes relaxation to become the norm, and without daily stress, we naturally broaden our field of vision. We become aware of greater reality."

"Lang, your perspective is too technical. Bree looks as though she's trying to translate the Egyptian Book of the Dead. It's really quite simple, Bree. When we were born to this life, we agreed to certain rules. One was to start with a clean slate. No recollection of prior existence or past accomplishments or mistakes. If reincarnation is a reality, and I believe it is, then being born with all that baggage would make life confusing at best. The next rule was that of time and space. Nowhere else but on Earth do we experience the passage of time; and without time there is no space. For example, if there were no time, then it would take me no time to cross the Atlantic bound for Europe. With no time, I would simply think of Europe and find myself there. But we agreed to live life within the confines of these accepted rules. We grow old in time and die. Death is simply a shedding, if you will, of the human body, a physical or earthly vehicle which houses our essence."

"Essence, Meredith? You're beginning to sound like me."

"Spirit, then. When we dispose of this body, we have nothing in which to live in a totally physical dimension. Our surroundings are not physical, and the key creator then becomes pure thought."

"Meredith is trying to tell you that your parents didn't actually go anywhere, Bree. They simply changed vibration and exist in a complimentary reality. It is a life of joy and a sense of belonging and love. Advanced meditators experience this phenomena regularly, having tapped into their higher dimension. But it is a reality you have not trained yourself to see. Not yet, anyway."

"And when does my training begin?"

"Why don't we start tomorrow with some meditation techniques. Considering the late hour, I am afraid we would all just fall asleep. I know I would. Is Bree's training the reason you want to move to Calvert, Meredith?"

"Not exactly, Lang. As you said, it's late. Let's continue this tomorrow."

So ended my first day in beautiful, quiet Calvert. I had no idea what was in store for me in this sleepy little town and beyond. How could I know or, for that matter, understand the role I would play in so many lives. At that moment, it didn't seem to matter. My comfort level had never been this high. It was a surprise to find myself in a town previously foreign to me, which could not have felt more like home.

# Chapter 2

The next morning, I awoke enticed out of a comfortable warm bed by the brilliant rising sun. A second-story veranda extended past a set of French doors outside my bedroom, and I found myself on it admiring the beautifully colored sunrise. The veranda overlooked a masterfully planted garden. The multicolored flowers admiringly leaned into the sunshine. I didn't know Wisconsin could be this beautiful. It had been years since I greeted the day with such enthusiasm. Dressed and ready, I quietly went to find the library I had glimpsed on my way through the house the evening before. Someone in this house was an avid reader. The room might not have had any walls. All one could see were books. There were books on every imaginable subject, grouped by subject and then alphabetized by author, then by title. From the classics to humor, American and European history, several dictionaries in a variety of languages, books on art and science, and a group devoted soley to religions and philosophy. The lack of books on psychic phenomena struck me as odd. This library was so complete; it seemed as though they were purposely omitted. I made a mental note to question Bree about the missing representation. Time passes quickly when one is engrossed in books. Once again, Meredith broke the silence.

"Lang, there you are. For a minute I was worried you were on your way home! I couldn't find you anywhere. Of course, this house is so large, hiding is no problem."

"I don't intend to run away or hide, Meredith. You have my curiosity in check. Certainly I cannot leave without knowing why I have been summoned here in the first place."

"There's that word again. Summoned."

"I know, I know; you prefer 'Destiny.' Must you be so dramatic?"

"Let's go in to breakfast, Lang. Bree is waiting." Arm in arm we strolled into the dining room.

"Good morning, Lang. How did you sleep?"

"Very well, thank you, Bree."

"Cafe au lait and croissants was my father's favorite breakfast. I hope you will enjoy it. Please help yourselves. The preserves are freshly made from fruit in the gardens."

"Bree, I hoped you wouldn't mind, but I availed myself of your library this morning. I was curious about the lack of books on psychic phenomena. Someone obviously gave thought to extending the contents of the library to nearly every subject; why omit the psychic realm?"

"You know, Lang, not everyone shares our fascination with the paranormal."

"That's true, Meredith; but somehow in this house of antiquity, I expected to find some sort of reference to the spiritual disciplines."

"The library was my father's personal domain, Lang. Mother

and I were allowed to use it, but had little influence over selected volumes. Father, unfortunately, felt anyone interested in psychic phenomena was delusional.

Consequently, nothing representing this subject was ever included in the library. It's odd considering my part in our proposal to you."

"Proposal, yes, I had nearly forgotten. What exactly is that proposal, Bree?"

"Fields University is located just outside of downtown Calvert. Perhaps you've heard of it?"

"Certainly, Fields is a private university with a fine reputation."

"The community has expressed an interest in adding a parapsychology department to Fields. I found out about this and because of my personal interest in progressing my own ability, I offered to fund the university for this department. That's the reason I was in Virginia auditing your class at Hardwick. It was suggested to me that you would be the perfect selection for a department head. After I had gotten to know Meredith, I discussed it with her. She seemed to feel there was more involved here than a simple career move."

"That's right, Lang. I haven't been able to pinpoint it, but something is evolving and this place is where it all will happen. I wish I could be more specific. From the look on your face, I see you wish I could be more specific! All I can say is that this move could change your life dramatically, and others as well. And, after all, your own department, the first of its kind in the Midwest, certainly that has some appeal."

"I want to see the university. Could we go now?" Meredith looked as though I had begun to speak in tongues. "Are you surprised, Meredith? You're not the only one with developed insight, you know. I'll get my coat."

Meredith and Bree virtually leaped from their seats, anxious to start for Fields lest I change my mind, no doubt.

"I must admit, Lang, you never cease to amaze me!"

"Well, let's go. What are we waiting for? Lang, you will love the campus. I'll call for the car." Bree looked delighted with the prospect of our beginning adventure.

We conversed happily as we enjoyed a splendid ride to Fields. Did she say I would love the campus? It was the most elegant architectural masterpiece. Massive white Gothic buildings sprawled over acres of perfect rolling landscape. Enormous chestnut trees scattered between buildings hosted happy squirrels gathering nuts, chattering, playing, and preparing for winter. Brilliant scarlet color splashed about in the form of burning bushes, offering a magnificent ornamental contrast to the stark white buildings. I had walked into the town of my dreams, the school of my dreams. No doubt my house waited to be discovered just around the corner.

"I called President Stepton this morning, Lang. He is very anxious to meet you. He should be in his office now," Bree explained as she pointed us in the proper direction down the corridor.

The president of Fields University, Martin Stepton, sidestepped any formal introduction and made me feel at ease. "Professor Evans, I am so happy we finally meet. The prospect of this department is all anyone is talking about around here. Please, look over the campus and we will set up a meeting to work out the details. Meredith provided us with your credentials and references, and I have to tell you that we would be honored to have you on staff. That is, if you are interested in making this move."

"If someone had told me a month ago that I would be relocating to the Midwest and working at a new university, I would have told them they were dead wrong. Now, I feel this not only a possibility, but a probability."

"I have also heard of your talent, Professor. Are you having some sort of paranormal reaction to all of this?" The look on this kind old gentleman's face was a mixture of curiosity and confusion. I smiled and asked that he might consider auditing a class in his new department.

For many it's hard to imagine that there is a way to experience life through other than the familiar five senses. Obviously, Dr. Stepton was completely unfamiliar with the field of study he was about to introduce to the university's students. I had to applaud him on keeping an open mind.

The next few weeks fairly flew by. I did manage to find a wonderful warm flat within walking distance of Field's. Meredith created an opportunity to open a New Age counseling center, combining her talent and her sociology degree to expertly guide those who sought her help. She busily and cheerfully began establishing herself in her new community. Before we realized it, things had settled and we fell into our expected routines. Hardwick lost a professor, but gained a competent replacement. I felt a little remorseful about leaving the school to which I had devoted ten years of my life. Worse, it seemed, they were relieved at my moving! Things at Hardwick would retreat into a nonthreatening mode. Surely, their precious budget was safe from the outrageous ideas of Professor Evans! It was difficult to think that all the work I had done at that institution went unappreciated. Ah, but Fields, on the other hand, was like a knowledge-hungry child, eager to evolve in the world of the paranormal, and it was a refreshing change.

I met my students the first day of class and was delighted with the reception I received. To my astonishment, a group of fifty-two students greeted me as I walked in the door. But a handful almost immediately struck a sense of recognition. Mark was a psychology major. He was skeptical about parapsychology, but curious.

"Curiosity leads to ever-expanding awareness, Mark. If you follow with an open mind, I am certain you will gain insight beyond your expectations."

"I must admit, Professor Evans, I'm looking forward to this class."

"What do you intend to teach in this course, Professor?"

The young woman who sat before me, not unlike Bree, was visibly consumed with unresolved issues. Her aura, fragmented and unhealthy, was misrepresented by the vibrant expectant expression on her young face, a disguise she apparently donned with ease. I also sensed her abilities on which, I suspected, she depended heavily for the survival of her psyche. "Alexandra, is it?" I simply called her name as it flashed through my mind. She seemed unaffected by the fact that I knew her name with no prompting.

"Yes, sir. But Alex, please."

"All right, Alex. I intend exactly what you anticipate, Alex!" The rest of the class looked a bit astonished with this response. What kind of an answer was that? What they did not perceive was the psychic ability and its casual use which was a natural part of Alex's communication skills. Her attempt to hide this fact from me was some sort of test of my own ability. She smiled an impish grin and nodded in response.

"For the rest of you who are true novices to this field, we will be studying various forms of awareness. We will start with meditation, which will be practiced daily. For the first week, we will have an expert in the field of meditation teach a method you will be comfortable with. You will also be monitored for a time until I am satisfied that you have grasped the concept and the mechanics of meditation. Then I would like for us to meet as a group on a daily basis to meditate together prior to classes. For this we have been offered the fine arts theater to comfortably accommodate our efforts with room for additional classes. This practice will have a two-fold purpose. First, meditation prepares you for the things you are about to learn and hopefully experience. Second, meditation in groups is far more effective and powerful than when individually practiced. Efficiency is often displayed through expediency and so you will see your abilities blossoming at a good pace with the help of your classmates. As we become comfortable with meditation, we will begin to add other dimensions to our awareness. We will study the classic extrasensory perception, go on to remote viewing, astral projection, channeling, and energy manipulation. Any subject within the realm of psychic awareness, which may have a special appeal to you, we will discuss and possibly pursue in this class. I want to streamline the class to your tastes and interests. At this time, I would like to introduce you to Ms. Gabrielle Lambeau. A graduate of Fields herself, she has funded the university for this study and will be auditing the course.

I would also like to introduce you to a very good friend of mine, Ms. Meredith Tolworth. Meredith is a long-time student of the occult, as well as a sociologist, teacher, and counselor of the New Age disciplines. You may be familiar with the New Age Counseling Center she has recently opened."

Directing my attention to Alex, I continued: "I mention this to you because in your pursuit of extrasensory knowledge and personal evolution, you may find this organization beneficial."

"Professor Evans, my name is Louis." This young man offered his name to me quickly and nervously in the apparent hope that I would not be delving into the private territory of his mind. "Will we be able to predict the future when we are done with this course?"

"The term 'predicting the future', Louis, leaves us with the assumption that one has no control over one's future. When you are done with this course, I hope you will be creatively directing your future. Yes, the young lady in the back row."

"Thank you, Professor. My name is Amy. What do you mean by directing your future?"

"You will learn just how powerful and creative you are as human beings. This, Ladies and Gentlemen, is an adventure into the very nature and creative energy of your psyche. We are venturing forth to explore the essence of creation. Essence is the life force of each of us. We have only to tap into this source to unleash that which is our birthright. Each and every one of you is a little piece of the power that created you. And as the true beneficiary of this power, you have abilities harnessed only by the limits of your imaginations."

"Professor Evans, my name is Mark. Is this some sort of religion you are teaching?"

"No, Mark, what I will teach you goes far beyond the confines of religion as we know it. You will learn truth beyond what you see with your eyes or hear with your ears. I do not promote, nor do I dissuade, organized religion. I do, however, encourage you to explore your true nature."

That first day will be etched in detail in my memory forever. The beginning, fresh, young, eager students with a propensity for enriching their lives. This would be the class I had waited for. These were the people who would benefit most from what I had to teach, and some would carry on the work.

Meredith, Bree, and I had dinner that evening to discuss plans and check on Bree's progress with meditation. We chose a small quaint restaurant in downtown Calvert. As usual our discussion leaned toward Bree's quest to become spiritually aware.

"I understand you're anxious for a dramatic experience, Bree. But first things first! Any noted changes in your meditation?"

"I experience a sensation of traveling, Lang. I don't see any specific place, but I do see color. But all the while, I feel as though I am moving, not just sitting relaxed in a chair. What does that mean? Is it my imagination?"

"It's a sign that you are following your path, Bree. You are progressing nicely, being prepared." This last remark evoked a puzzled look for response. Just the reaction I was looking for. "Meredith was telling me you will be doing some work at the counseling center."

"I was thrilled she asked me. My degree is in social work, as is Meredith's; but I never applied it to a career. I hope I will be effective."

Having thrown herself into her student career after losing her parents, Bree graduated with honors. However, she never recognized or applied her exceptional education. "I chose Fields, not because of its academic reputation, but because it meant I could remain in the house I loved and grew up in. I never thought much about a career."

"You will be wonderful, Bree. You worked so hard for your education, Calvert will benefit from your knowledge and especially your caring attitude. I was hoping, if it's not too much trouble, that you might join the class for meditation each morning. I would like to establish this routine as soon as possible, before classes start for the day. How does 7A.M. sound to you?"

"Early! But I will be there, Lang. I remember your mentioning that meditation is more effective in groups. I want to progress this as quickly as possible."

"Then it will be done!" We laughed over an exaggerated handshake and cinched our deal.

As the weeks went by, it became obvious to me that this class was well suited to the subject as well as to each other. I had high hopes for all of them, in whatever field they chose to pursue. It was clear to me that as a group they were beginning to display signs of blossoming awareness.

Meditation, in particular, was shaping attitudes. I watched these young adults mature emotionally, calmly, intuitively. This was certainly what my work was about. A handful of the students had begun to meet weekly, outside of class, at the counseling center. We were becoming a family, beginning to sense each other's moods and feelings. These subtle changes strengthened my belief in what I taught. I was getting feedback from other professors and family members on the positive changes in all of the students. Confidence, awareness, a quiet strength, all wonderful qualities attributed to the disciplines of the contemplative art we call meditation. I could not have been more proud of this group if they had been my own children.

At a meeting at the counseling center, I was asked a question I had been expecting for some time. "Professor Lang, what brought you into this field?" The question I expected came from Mark. He was a natural and was nearly consuming information. A psychology major, as I was, I saw myself in him at his age. Eager to learn at a point where possibilities were unfolding almost too rapidly to be acknowledged consciously.

"Mark, I was in childhood, adolescence, and young adulthood what I laughingly referred to as accidentally psychic. As a child, I would experience a precognitive dream, and then days later watch it unfold; I thought everyone experienced the same phenomena in their lives. It seemed normal to me. Episodes of deja vu, astral dreams and clairaudience became common throughout my life, although initially uncontrollable. My first interest was in psychology. I was reminded on a regular basis how irregular and unpopular my episodes of psychic awareness were. At first I saw it as a handicap. Surely, it would slip out among my colleagues, and there I would be, labeled as some sort of lunatic in their midst. I really felt quite sorry for myself until I had a flash of inspiration. What if there were unseen teachers, who needed someone such as me to establish their credibility? How could they teach something as difficult as continued awareness through someone with little or no education? It would be as if Einstein were trying to communicate continued and unfolding scientific data through a five year old. I realized then that I could not allow colleagues to stifle the gifts I had been given. Rather, I had to develop all that I could, at whatever cost and more importantly, find others like me to carry on this noble profession. Others including you, Mark."

"You see talent in me that I have not discovered yet?"

"In fact, I do. The science that is closest to what we are endeavoring to experience is Physics. It has already proven several things scientifically that previously were considered products of fertile imaginations. One of the more interesting discoveries is that objects we consider solid and real, such as this oak table, when reduced to a subatomic level become nothing more than swirling matter. This is the same information given us by mystics down through the centuries. Physics, essentially, has its hand on the doorknob of the door of truth. If what we consider to be real is simply molecules in motion, then our search to experience true reality will lead us to heretofore unimagined, unlimited knowledge and experiences. This is a frontier, my young friends. Something new and different, which in reality is older than time itself, and ultimately will lead us home to our true nature and birthright.

But I digress. Meredith, I've been meaning to ask, why are you collecting photos of missing children?"

"Collecting? No, these come in the mail. I . . . I don't know; I just haven't been able to throw them out. I feel I know the children, or would know them if I saw them. I somehow feel connected to these kids. I know I can't change anyone's process of learning, but somehow I . . . I just feel connected. I must keep these. I can't throw them out."

She seemed to be speaking more to herself than addressing anyone in the room. "Meredith, you are pale, Dear. Please, sit down." Her expression I could only describe as detached. I was familiar with that look, that dismembered speech pattern. What path was this woman planning to follow? At that moment, I knew I would be involved, but how?

# Chapter 3

Out-of-body experience, the art of detaching one's spirit and traveling without the encumbrance of a physical body, was natural to me. I would find myself in the strangest places, talking to people I did not know, not in this world, anyway. Sometimes, I consciously directed these travels; other times I seemed to just float about indiscriminately. One night, I don't know, on a whim maybe, I decided to try something I was taught through the infinite wisdom and patience of an Eastern mystic. I decided to try to awaken the astral bodies of some of my students and take them on a "guided tour of dreams." I was first drawn to Mark. As I thought of him, I instantly found myself standing at the foot of his bed, watching him as he peacefully slept. I closed my eyes and imagined his spirit rising out of his body. A sensation of warmth came over me, and I opened my eyes to find a startled young man standing before me.

Looking solid and real, I looked past him to find his physical body still lying in a contented sleep in his bed. I smiled and nodded to him as he turned to find his body lying asleep.

"Don't be alarmed, Mark. I thought we might do some exploring. You have projected your spirit from your body. It shall sleep on until you return safely to it. Shall we see if we can draw Alex, as well?" The thought barely expressed, we were instantly standing in the room where Alex slept; and once again, a startled but detached spirit stood in front of us. It was important for me to establish communication and reassure her, lest she fearfully snap herself back into her body.

"Alex, you are not dreaming. You're in an astral state. You're perfectly safe. Would you care to take a little trip with us?"

Before too long, Amy, Louis, and Meredith all joined our experimental group. And then, the strangest thing; we were talking, sitting around a large round table we created for comfort's sake when suddenly we seemed to lose control. Shapes melted and swirled about us. As though some unseen force propelled us through space, we moved unaware of our impending destination. Was this a part of the destiny Meredith spoke of? Did we somehow agree to an experience that would take complete control? Had we agreed to allow the drama to unfold unaided by its participants? I was no more in control than any of the others, but somehow I had to keep them from becoming alarmed.

"Where are we? What's going on?" Mark spoke, panic mounting in his voice, like an unhappy passenger on an amazing carnival ride.

"It's all right, Mark. We're all together. If you need to, you can return to your body at any time. You are in no danger, I assure you. But I think it's best we allow this to continue and find out where we are to be led and why."

In the midst of the speech I was giving, I noticed a faint noise in the background. Our perpetual motion had stopped. The sound was sobbing. A child sobbing, but I needed to focus on our surroundings and establish where we were.

"Meredith. Where are you? Can you hear the child?"

"I hear her, Lang. I see her, as well. Follow the sound of her voice. Good, now turn and face me."

With that the room lit up. A small, sparsely furnished room with a single bed, a plain dresser, one window, one door, a very frightened little blonde girl. "This is it, Lang. This is why we were all brought together. The children, lost children." Meredith's voice cracked with emotion at this realization. A look of joy came over her beautiful face. "We are caretakers of lost children. Do you realize the honor, not to mention the responsibility?"

The child seemed to know she was not alone. She stopped crying and looked up just as Meredith stepped in front of her. "You can see me, Little One. Don't be frightened, you're not alone. We will help you."

"Are you an angel?" the child asked innocently.

"Angel? O.K., right . . . we're angels!" Mark looked more bewildered than he did earlier when we started this journey. "How can she see us?"

"Children use their natural ability until a grown-up advises them against exercising their overactive imaginations." It wasn't my best explanation, but my attention was drawn to the child sitting on the bed looking so lost and small. I approached her. "What's your name, Dear?"

"Annette. I want my mommy!" And the tears returned.

"Of course, Honey. That's why we're here. We will help get you back to your mommy."

✒

We explained that not everyone could see us. She seemed to accept that willingly. "Of course not, you're angels. You have to be in bad trouble to see angels!"

"Right! That's right! We're angels! So, angels, how do we get her out of here?" Louis was nervously caught up, as we all were, in the impact of a mission for which we were completely unprepared. Suddenly thrust upon us was the opportunity and the ability to save this child.

Annette started to relax and began to chatter. "The lady said she would buy me ice cream and that she was a friend of Mommy's; but we drove so long I fell asleep. When I woke up, I was here. I can't open the door." And tears began to well in her eyes once again. "I want my mommy!" She started to sob.

I was afraid someone outside this room might hear her. We didn't want to wake anyone while we formulated a plan. Mark, taken with the plight of this child, spoke first: "Why don't we just take her home?"

"Right, Mark, did you bring your car?"

"Well, you don't have to get sarcastic, Alex!"

"Stop it. Don't waste energy arguing. We can do this; we just have to be creative about it. We are in a nonphysical state; consequently, moving physical objects can't be done in the usual way. However, if we blend our energy and focus, I believe we can use psychokinesis effectively. Join hands and concentrate on the lock on that door. We have to get this child out of here before someone wakes up."

I sounded like I knew what I was talking about, but this was as bewildering to me as it was to any of them. That would have to be my little secret. No, by the look on Meredith's face, I saw it was our little secret. "Concentrate on that lock; see it heat up, turn red, and melt. Come on now, we can do this!"

It didn't seem to be working. Were we trying too hard?

"O.K., we have to relax and let this happen naturally. Meredith, any suggestions?"

"Yes, Lang. Create the element that will melt the lock first."

"Of course; heat, it's so simple! Imagine heat as glowing energy in concentrated form. Now form it into a ball, like a ball of fire. Now move it toward the door, now the lock, and . . ." It was working. We all saw the lock heat up as if being manipulated by an ironworker about to reshape it. The mechanism gave and rendered the lock useless.

"Annette." The child looked up at me drying her tears. "Honey, we need your help. Open the door. It's not locked anymore, but be careful not to touch the lock; it's hot."

She did as she was told. Amy spoke softly to the child, looking for a wrap. "Do you have a coat, Annette?"

"I did, but the lady took it when she left."

"Never mind, Dear. Take that blanket and wrap it around yourself." She did as she was told, but being so small, the blanket was a lot to handle. Amy watched with an approving smile as the small child struggled to wrap herself in the large blanket. "Good, now stand back while we check outside."

The hallway was dimly lit and poorly maintained. We were in some third-rate hotel. No one lurked in the hall. I waved an "all clear" and the child, surrounded by her "angels" moved out of the room, down the hall, down the staircase, and into the street. We were in a large city. Tall buildings loomed and encircled us, giving an almost surrealistic quality aided by the artificially lit night. I had no idea where we were or how to get my bearings. Mark, fortunately, recognized his surroundings. "Chicago! We're in Chicago!"

"I'm glad you know where you are, Mark. Personally, I'm lost. Where would we most likely run into a police officer? We need to get Annette to someone trustworthy who can successfully complete this journey for us."

"That's State Street ahead. We are bound to run into a beat cop on a main street. Let's just follow it through to downtown."

"Good. Let's go."

Homeless people, half-asleep on benches and doorways, must have sworn to give up drinking as they watched a small child wrapped in a pink blanket skipping past them down the street. Occasionally, one would call out to her, or try to grab her as she ran past. Auras surrounding these people were more prominent to us than their physical appearances. It was an eerie sight in this already strange environment, but it was beneficial. Seeing their auras clearly allowed us to determine who the kind souls were. But most important, we were able to determine those from whom to distance the child. By the appearance of their muddied oppressive energies, we knew who might potentially harm her.

"Just keep going, Annette; move a little faster. We're here with you. We won't let anything happen to you." Alex was right behind her, and seemed determined to protect her at all costs.

Annette was a brave little girl, and we guided her through the streets on a safe path. "There, Annette, see the man in the blue uniform?" Alex exclaimed excitedly. "He will help us. When we get to him, tell him you are lost and want to go home."

"O.K.!" Our little ward cheerfully picked up speed and darted toward her rescuer. The officer turned to see a child running toward him nearly tripping over the blanket she held around herself. His aura, for at this point with our precious Annette we could afford to trust no one, was white with splashes of sky blue. He was a bear of a man. The gentle crystalline energy lovingly swirling around him told us this was a man with a heart, a man we could trust.

"Not so fast! And where will you be going in the middle of the night, Missy?" He reached out and scooped up the child in two big arms, holding her strongly to him. A feeling of warmth descended over us all as we watched this child regain her confidence. The officer defied his stature and obvious masculinity as he showed his nurturing side, eliciting trust from this innocent little girl. It was a touching scene. Annette was safe, and she knew it; we all knew it.

"The angels said I should tell you I want to go home to Mommy. Will you take me?"

"Angels, is it? Well, of course I will!"

Annette was on her way home.

And the "angels" returned with no further delay to our respective beds, sound asleep.

The next day was Saturday and our small group was in the habit of meeting at the counseling center, determined not to interrupt our daily meditation. But this morning's meditation time gave way to comic relief. Mark started to relate a dream he had the night before. I couldn't resist sitting back and watching all of this unfold.

"You'll never believe this dream. We were all together, but we were asleep . . . I think! Anyway, we ended up in this dingy hotel in Chicago and found this missing kid and . . ." At this point, Mark noticed the curious, bewildered looks on the faces of his friends. "You," he pointed to Alex, "got on my case because I wanted to take this little girl home, but we weren't really there, and we didn't know how we were going to do it. You asked me if I had brought my car. O.K., what's going on here?"

Alex spoke next. "I had the same dream. I remember asking if you had brought your car; and Professor Evans, you were there!"

"Really?" I feigned mild curiosity, trying to hide my enjoyment.

Amy continued. "You told us to concentrate on melting the lock on the door. It didn't work at first, but . . ."

Realizing they were all in the same "dream", they finally looked my way. They were all completely confused. I could no longer contain my laughter. "It's all right. Really! You were astral projecting. We really were in Chicago last night. All of us, all together."

"And that little girl, Annette, was she there, too?"

"Look for yourself, Louis." Meredith had entered the room, carrying a copy of the Chicago Sun Times. The paper headlined an amazing story:

MISSING GIRL RETURNED HOME WITH THE HELP
OF ANGELS!

The looks on their faces were priceless. A more perplexed group could not have existed. I was beginning to feel sorry for them. Well, not really. Truthfully, I was enjoying this too much. "It's all right, honestly!"

"We've discussed for months the possibility of experiencing life through awareness not linked to our physical selves. Well, last night, we did."

A flood of questions all came at me at once. "One at a time, people, please."

"How did we get to Chicago if we were all asleep?"

"Have you been asleep during my lectures on astral projection, Mark?"

"No,Sir, but I never expected to be able to do it! I mean, it works? Really works?"

"Yes, Mark. It really works; and we were able to return a child to safety. I would say we had a wonderful, productive experience, wouldn't you?"

Meredith spoke, bringing a serious note to our lighthearted conversation. "It's not over, Lang. There are more."

"More?"

"Yes, Lang. There are more children needing our help. That's why we were all brought together. We must pursue this in order to help the lost children. There are many for whom being abducted or just lost was an accident. It had nothing to do with their spiritual growth and we must find them. Return them to where they belong and to the people who love them."

Alex looked perplexed, obviously thinking about the magnitude of this concept. "Surely we have no ability to find all the missing kids in this world."

"No, Alex, but what Meredith means is that for some, being removed from their homes was not part of their planned experience in this life. We choose to experience many things in the course of lifetimes, in order to become better, stronger, more loving, more informed beings. To this end, we create. But sometimes by concentrating on things brought about by fear, an inordinate amount of attention, we create by default. Things that have no bearing on our growth or awareness happen accidentally."

"That's right," Meredith added. "And we can help."

"We will help, Meredith."

# Chapter 4

"I don't get it. What does "create by default" mean, exactly?"

"Remember our first day of class, Louis? You asked if I would be teaching you how to predict the future?"

"Right, and you said something about directing the future. I didn't understand then, either."

"Well, Louis, it's simple. We chose this experience to become more evolved beings. We are in control of all things we experience, good and bad. Sometimes, the bad things teach us lessons and allow us to gain strength in ways unobtainable through any other method. Consequently, we are the masters of our own destinies. However, until we come to understand that we are in control, we sometimes cause things to happen just by focusing attention on them. And sometimes, these things can be detrimental to our physical and/or mental well-being. In other words, we create by default."

"How, Professor Evans?" Amy seemed beyond understanding.

"First, you must realize that everything in your life is under your control, and that what you think is reality in a sort of pre-birthing stage. The more attention you give to an idea, the more emotion you enhance it with, the more chance you have of bringing it into your life."

"Certainly no one wants any child to be kidnapped."

"No, Amy; but the constant fear we sometimes show toward a possibility gives it substance, giving it its own energy, and by mistake, we create or draw what we fear."

"Just by giving it attention."

"Yes."

"Just by thinking about something, I can cause it to happen."

"Yes and no."

"Now I'm really confused!"

"I can see that. All right, Amy; let's start over. Obviously a passing thought does not turn instantly into reality. Otherwise statements like 'I could just die!' would result in our instant demise. However, thoughts are forms of energy. They have substance. Just as we cannot see radio or television waves that bring sound and picture, nevertheless, they exist. Thought is such energy and over time will reduce itself to matter becoming what we experience as conscious reality."

"So, if you're really afraid something bad may happen to you, you actually can make it happen by thinking and worrying about it all the time."

"Yes. And conversely, you can bring good things into your life by thinking and planning for them."

"You're kidding!"

"Why, Alex, is this so difficult for you to accept?"

"I don't know. I guess I thought most things happen by accident."

"They can, but they are accidents that you create by . . ."

"I know, I know, by default."

"Yes! Unfortunately, most of us are taught to deal with whatever life throws at us. The truth is, you are in complete control. It is what you do with that control that will ultimately shape your destiny."

Mark's look was one of disbelief. "Professor Evans, that's all very interesting; but you cannot believe that poor little Annette kept fearfully visualizing her abduction until it happened."

"Not likely, Mark; but her parents may have inadvertently fed this fear. Or others in her circle of family, friends or neighbors who were constantly re-creating their worst nightmare by reading articles of other abductions, or hearing them described on the news, or feeling the desolation of how they would react if such a thing happened to a child they have grown to love. The world we choose to live in, the one we focus our attention on, is the one that is reality for each of us. There is room for all our hopes and fears."

"This is too deep for me."

"Maybe so, Amy; but think about it. When we realize we have control, we react at first with fear and an overwhelming sense of responsibility. But possibilities become unlimited, and the world becomes an artist's canvas waiting for creation, rather than a place full of dread and helplessness."

"Then, when we ask why God would bring hunger or disease into this world . . ."

"We brought the hunger and the disease. Just break down and analyze the word disease. It is 'dis-ease,' implying not being at ease with one's self which causes a physical malfunction. Hunger or the lack of anything multiplies from our constant awareness of that lack. We have free will and the ability to create, and with this ability we fashion our belief system from which we affirm what we see as truth." I was beginning to think I would need a drill to get this idea through. "Believe what you will, but if you are honest with yourselves, you will see evidence in your everyday lives of your own powers of creation. The reason we find this so hard to accept is because once we have accepted it, we can no longer blame another for things that happen in our lives. It is absolute personal power with which goes absolute personal responsibility."

"Oh, that word!" Alex crinkled her nose.

"That's right, Alex. That's the real fear. Accepting responsibility."

And so the Angels were formed. A group brought together for the sole purpose of rescuing and returning missing children. Was this some sort of coincidence? Did we all meet by accident? Or were Meredith and I guided somehow in bringing these young people into a drama that would change their lives forever? Personally, I do not believe in coincidence. Considering the success of the Angels, their creative determination and obvious intention to help children, it would be difficult for me to assume this was some sort of unplanned fortuitous accident. Life has taught me on many occasions that things are rarely unplanned.

Allow me to introduce you to the group, without whose efforts none of this would be a reality.

I will start with Alexandra. Tall, all arms and legs, with red hair to match her flaming temper. Tough, unspoiled, a bit too quick to react, that's our Alex. Her home life was less than storybook. Certainly because of her unfortunate background, she turned to Meredith for counseling. That was her best choice.

She would never entirely abandon her rough exterior, the granite wall surrounding her that protected raw emotion, her quick-to-judge attitude. Her use of sarcasm had become legendary throughout the university. But we knew underneath the armor she wore through life was a gentle, caring, often frightened

creature who was prone to abundant self-protection. Had someone given her the attention she deserved as a child, she would not
need to make up for the lack of it. But lessons come in all forms.
We loved and cared for Alex as part of our family, a new experience for which she needed time to adjust. Alexandra was an aster-
isk in the lives of a prominent political family. Her upbringing
was left to the domestic help and to schools paid exorbitant
amounts of money to keep her. Family life was foreign to Alex. As
a result, from her perspective, everyone had an angle, an agenda.
It was her job to suspect every human that entered the perimeter
of her life and to determine just exactly what he or she wanted,
preferably before they had a chance to utter a first word.

A strange environment for the tender development of psychic
awareness, but just as some flowers grow stubbornly between
slabs of concrete, so did Alex's intuitive ability. As a child, Alex
experienced dreams, not unlike mine, which turned out to be precognitive. In addition, she seemed to have an uncanny sense of
death. This did nothing to assuage her feelings of estrangement.
She seemed unusually drawn to the company of someone who
was about to depart from this world. At a very young age, Alex
would show an enormous interest in such individuals.

Since her natural personality did not exhibit traits of overt
friendliness, it was often noticed when she would go out of her
way to slip her hand into another's, or offer an unsolicited hug.
Whether anyone in her immediate family caught on is unknown.
But as the years went by, it became apparent to Alexandra herself
that when she felt the need to be in the company of certain individuals, she was actually saying good-bye, for it was often only a
matter of a few weeks before they made their respective journeys
into the next world.

For a sensitive child, this realization could be no less than
shattering. She was obviously unwanted, and knew it. Rarely did

family visit at school. The invitations to plays and concerts were ignored by her parents. She had no recollection of them attending even one. Then to be an unwilling co-messenger of death ended any thought, in her own mind, of becoming a valued family member.

Such a heavy secret for a little girl. The need to say good-bye next manifested itself in a spectacular dream. An uncle who tried to give Alex some attention, probably realizing she was seriously lacking in affection, harbored a more caring spirit than those of the rest of her family. This uncle died rather young, while seemingly in good health. Ten days before his untimely death, Alex had a dream.

She was eight years old at that time, and the dream was a beautiful one, not sinister at all. Walking side by side through a field of wildflowers, she took her uncle's hand. At the end of the path, they stopped to watch something descending from the sky. According to Alex's description, it was a sack made of a thick black material, holding mysterious weighty contents that rounded it out at the bottom. The material was gathered and held tightly closed by unseen hands, forming a bulbous, burdened makeshift container.

As they stood and gazed at the dense black ball protruding from the sky, they anticipated the treasure it held. Then, unexpectedly, the hands released one end of the material to scatter its contents.

The inside of the cloth revealed a rich velvet nap and spilled in folds releasing sizable chunks of glistening purple objects, which turned out to be thousands of highly polished, brilliant purple amethysts. Alex stooped to pick an especially beautiful one and turned to hand it to her favorite uncle. At that point, still dreaming, she realized the stone was a gift, and that she would not see him again. Then she awoke.

Ten days later, in a hotel in a strange city far from home, Alex's uncle passed on. No one in her family was there to hold his hand, or to say good-bye. But Alex knew that she had said good-bye to him in the dream. And he had a beautiful amethyst to remember her by.

Other dreams portending death interrupted the child's sleep. She would dream of losing teeth. A strange dream for a child, surely; but in the dream she would panic and hold the tooth in her little hand, looking desperately for someone to help her fix her tooth so that it was back securely in her mouth. But she never found the help, and once again would awaken in a state of panic.

She came to realize that within weeks, a month at the most, someone known to her would pass on. Whether or not the person was someone to whom she felt a bond was signified by how alarmed she was in the dream, and how desperately she tried to find help to replace her missing tooth. In dreams in which she took the loss casually the person was known to her, but not a family member or close friend. Possibly, Alex's own brush with death and the casual way she felt about the transition was the reason for her sensitivity to those about to cross over.

As a child, Alex's health was less than perfect. She was prone toward infections, debilitating allergies, and a less than responsive immune system. She seemed more often sick than well and often would contract unusual and untreatable ailments, rarely seen in one so young. She often told people, much to the dismay of her family, that she did not belong in this world and would probably leave it soon. The turning point in her health as well as her attitude, as Alex explains it, came over a period of six months.

Alex believes this was the time when she finally had to make her decision. The decision was to stay or to go. During this six-month period, Alex experienced a recurring dream. She does not call it a nightmare because it didn't frighten her. But as you read on, you will realize that most children would react to such a dream with fear.

What Alex did not apparently realize at the time, but is now aware of, was that the dream was not a dream at all. In reality, she was astral projecting.

The sequence of events, always playing out in the same fashion, would go like this. She would be sleeping in her bed. She was in a boarding school at the age of ten, and slept in a single bed in a very stark room. She would awaken, sit up, climb out of bed, and leave the room.

She walked into the hallway and turned to face a large arched alcove at the end of it. The alcove was a modified tiny indentation of a room with an arched entrance and seemed to become larger as she looked on. The bust of a man would appear. Able to see only his head and shoulders, he seemed to float in midair. This scene did not alarm Alex. She calmly stood and watched. As the altered figure floated, it seemed to beckon to her. It had no arms with which to beckon, but her feeling was that it wanted her to move closer. That she did, but at a certain point she would just stop and stare. Instinctively, to hear her tell it, she knew that this entity wanted her to follow him. She also knew that she could leave by crossing the threshold and passing through the arch. Had she done this, she believed she would never return.

For a period of six months, this dream and the visiting spirit in the alcove would haunt her. Two or three times a week, the child would journey, all alone, into the hallway and gaze at the spirit in the alcove. At the end of six months, Alex made a choice to stay. That was the last of her recurring dream.

Not that death was in any way foreign to her, or frightening. But she felt, on some level, that she had something yet to do in this world. And she determined that she had the strength to do it. And so she does. Alex is our defending knight. Often using her brusque demanding attitude to capture the attention of a wandering child, or to stave off one who might do the child harm frequently transcending her astral state. She has found her home and her family. The Angels are her family. Meredith, especially, has become her mentor. Alexandra's talent, being finely cultivated and guided by Meredith, will continue her work. She may become less antagonistic over the years, but Alex will never allow anyone to feel sorry for themselves. She will be their mentor of strength and perseverance. Aside from Bree, Alex is Meredith's favorite.

Amy was Alex's opposite. From a loving home with doting parents, the world was a fancy birthday cake to Amy. She loved everything and everyone. A spider would be gently coaxed into a glass and removed to the basement, where it could live out the rest of its days without the squashing interference of a marauding human. She saw life as the ultimate shrine and treated all its participants with equal respect. Diminutive and impish describes Amy's appearance, with dark hair and dark eyes. But as unassuming as she is, her caring ways have turned many a friend, family member, and teacher to understand the world of love she chooses to live in.

Amy's interests lie in the world of science. From biology to physics, her quest for knowledge is unquenchable. The fact that this future scientist would consider a class in the paranormal came as quite a shock to those who knew her best. Her explanation was that she intended to have as well rounded an education as possible, so that in trying to discover the secrets of the universe, she would have all intelligent thought at her disposal from which to experiment. Amy chooses to enrich her world as a thinker in possibility, not as one given boundaries of thought from which she can only draw finite conclusions. As for becoming one of the Angels, her feeling is that however she can help to make a life better, she will be there to do that.

Amy's psychic interests stemmed from her grandmother. A woman of great knowledge and equal strength, she spent much time with Amy from infancy on.

Amy lost her grandmother from the physical world when Amy was a student in high school. On the day of her grandmother's funeral, Amy returned home and headed for her room to be alone with her thoughts. She sat on the edge of her bed and said good-bye to the woman who meant so much to her. Although she felt a grievous loss, Amy was able to talk, feeling her grandmother was somehow there to listen. She asked for a sign. "Tell me, Grandma, that you are O.K. If I know that you are all right and happy, I will be happy, too."

Amy got that sign immediately. A cold November day, she opened her eyes to see a white butterfly flying toward her. The butterfly seemed to glow, and if that wasn't peculiar enough, it headed right for her face, in case it had not gotten her attention! She cupped her hands to catch it, wondering how a butterfly had survived a Wisconsin autumn, and why it glowed like a firefly. But when she looked in her hands, there was nothing there. She looked up and saw it resting on the edge of her dresser. As she walked toward it, the butterfly disappeared.

That night, as she prepared for bed, she heard three knocks on her closed bedroom door. Opening the door, Amy found no one there. Each night for a week, she heard the knocks as she prepared for bed, and each time she went to the door to find no one there. Finally, on the seventh night, she knelt at her bed and said a prayer for her grandmother. She also thanked her grandmother for the signs she received, and the knocks stopped. But Amy believes her grandmother watches over her, just as she did when she was a little girl. If she is worried or depressed, she will invariably smell her grandmother's perfume. She feels comforted by this sign, and happy that her grandmother visits her when she needs her most. Our Amy is the gentle one. Often comforting a frightened child as we determine how best to rescue him or her. She is our sweetest Angel.

Louis is the jock. His love of sports is obvious in his muscular appearance. But his attitude toward the children he helps shows a nature that is gentle and caring. Louis has no perceivable psychic gifts. In fact, until his first day in my class, he wasn't completely sure what parapsychology really was. From his standpoint of lack of knowledge, he is a veritable sponge. He can't seem to get enough information on the subject, and is an avid student. Since sports seemed to be his only interest, he feels a whole new world opened up for him after discovering my class. His ability to remember our astral trips is an unending source of wonder to him. He cannot deny the fact that they happen, yet he questions every aspect of how they can occur. He is completely shocked, every time, to learn that the experiences he feels are dreams, were dreamt by each of us at the same time, and that there is physical proof, often in the form of a newspaper article documenting our efforts, as we manage to save a child. On an intellectual level he understands the reality of his experiences, but on a conscious level he has trouble believing it's all real.

And yet, Louis's spirit, unencumbered by physical sensation and reason, is undeniably reliable in the astral state. He is often the first at the side of a lost child. His love of geography helps him to help us determine just where we are. His curiosity is a constant source of amusement to the rest of us. Louis will have the most incredible psychic experience, then question its validity from beginning to end. Just when we think he has asked every imaginable question, he comes up with another one.

Football has taken a backseat to finding missing children. This is perplexing to Louis's father, who envisioned his son as a future star athlete. Of course, his father is unaware of Louis's efforts as one of the Angels. And unfortunately, they have less of a relationship since Louis is no longer goal oriented in the field of sports. At times I think Louis misses that world. I have suggested to him that he could resume his football career and still remain to help with our cause. But he seems so joyously caught up in the blossoming world of the paranormal that he claims everything else is far less important to him.

And then there is Mark. A student of psychology, he feels the paranormal enhances his ability to understand people and their needs. I quite agree. Mark is tall and slender. He is described as bookish. His quiet demeanor and easygoing attitude is often put to the test when Louis and Alex lock horns. Mark takes on the role of mediator and peace reigns once again.

I have taken a personal interest in Mark's training. I believe he has psychic abilities he is not necessarily aware of. It has been effectual to point out to him, on different occasions, how his decisions were often made with his intuition at work. He is quite amazed at the outcomes of our astral "dreams," and many times has remarked how honored he is to be a member of our group.

His psychic awareness displays itself in past life recall. As a child, Mark recounts the story of being brought to the local natural history museum. He was quiet and would sometimes be left accidentally. His mother, turning to find he was left behind, would frantically begin searching the halls. Invariably, she would find Mark in front of old oil paintings of American Indians. There he would be, age four, so engrossed in the scene he stood before, so swept away by the emotion of recognition, that tears quietly and steadily descended down his cheeks. His mother was alarmed by these unusual reactions. Her response to the problem was to get him away from the paintings.

Having met with Jerry, an amazing teacher you will be introduced to later, Mark was told that his recollection was of a life as an American Indian and a shaman. The sadness stemming from this lifetime was due to the fact that the Indians were losing their land, their magnificent colorful life, and often their will to live. In his Indian incarnation as a healer, Mark fought valiantly to save the lives of his people, a battle he ultimately lost. Mark was so fascinated by the details of his past life, supplied to him by Jerry, that reincarnation became his primary area of study. It also became clear that his interest in Indian artifacts and ceremonial objects reflected memory, and these things became treasured mementos.

In this life as a psychologist, his knowledge of reincarnation will no doubt assist him in meeting the needs and solving the problems of his future patients.

And, of course, our Bree. Although she did not accompany us on our first out-of-body experience, Bree was destined to join the Angels. Upon hearing about our first adventure without her she felt a bit left out, but wanted all the details. I had purposely omitted Bree from our initial experiment.

I wanted to see if I had the ability to draw those who trusted me into an astral state. But Bree's first and most important journey would be too personal for her to share with a group. We filled her in on the experiment and assured her that her turn was coming. Was she ready for what she was about to experience? Goodness, this one I could not have anticipated. I should have been asking if I was ready.

"Tell me more, Lang, about this astral projection. Could you take me on a tour of dreams?"

"It would be my absolute pleasure, Lovely Lady."

"When?"

"Patience! Let's not thwart the element of surprise. I assure you, I will not forget. Trust me. You have been doing so well with meditation, I believe you are ready for an adventure."

"I want to see my parents, Lang. In meditation, I feel they are so close and yet I do not see them. Would astral projection help me to see my parents?"

"Only you can program this outing, my dear. If you have a true desire and it can override your fear, you will see them. Whatever you do, do not become discouraged. It will happen. And it will happen sooner than you expect, if you believe and devote energy to it. In the meantime, to prepare for this experience, imagine how all of you would react seeing each other again for the first time in so many years. Don't be afraid to feel the emotion of that reunion. You will give substance and energy to that meeting. Work at it, Bree. Make it a reality. You must do this for yourself. No one else could have the kind of emotional attachment and desire needed to accomplish this for you. Do you understand?"

"Yes, Lang, I think I do. In other words, my need to see them coupled with the love I feel for them will help me find my way into their world."

"That's it, Bree! Work at it. Make it happen. You have that power."

A night, unforgettable just in its natural splendor alone, was the backdrop for Bree's first experience with the astral state. It had been two weeks since our discussion with Bree and the instructions we left with her. It seemed she had been doing what she was told because both Meredith and I realized it was time.

Meredith and I both accompanied Bree on her first out-of-body experience. It was a trip filled with anticipation. As a result of Bree having done her homework, both Meredith and I were subconsciously and astrally drawn to her in the middle of the night to awaken her astral body from her sleep. This time, we stood at the foot of Bree's lavish Victorian canopy bed. The two of us imagined her standing before us, and yes, there she stood, in spirit while her body slept.

"Think of where you want to be, Bree. We will be right behind you." We tagged along more to encourage than anything else. This was Bree's experience. She orchestrated and directed all of it. She would be where her wish would be fulfilled, and only she knew how to get there.

A thought simply transferred and we found ourselves amidst the most intoxicating gardens.

"Look at these flowers. The colors are magnificent, like nothing I have ever seen." Bree's enchantment was infectious. The gardens were glorious. Flowers which, blooming in an earthly garden would have lived in separate seasons, all radiantly and gently swayed in a tranquil sweet breeze deluged with the combined scents of their individual perfumes. The intensity and brilliance of color was astounding, almost luminescent. They were vibrant reds, blues, greens, and yellows. Orchids and lilacs, tulips and roses, and hundreds of others too numerous to mention. A path wound through the gardens alongside a flowing stream of musically moving water. Carved footbridges gracefully crossed the water connecting one garden to the next.

"This is the type of place I have imagined my mother to be in. She so loved flowers." Words barely uttered by a loving daughter, a beautiful woman stood in the distance among the flowers, facing Bree. We all saw her. She was tall and slender, with Bree's burnished auburn hair. She turned and knelt to pick a flower, and as we watched, her face changed from young to mature and back to young again. She held the flower out toward Bree with one hand and extended her other arm as if in greeting. She was Bree's mother.

"Gabrielle." A lyrical voice called to Bree, and as though a statue was suddenly given life, Bree, finally realizing who she was looking at, flew into her mother's arms. Meredith and I felt like intruders on this touching scene, but we could not tear ourselves away. Besides, we had a purpose. We were emotional support.

"Mother. Is it really you?"

"Yes, my dearest. We never really left you. I have prayed to be able to tell you that. And finally my prayers are answered. We are as close to you as a thought." This beautiful woman gestured as she spoke in a style hinting of her European upbringing. A man approached. A tall, dark, handsome Frenchman. The sight of him was almost more than Bree could bear.

"Papa!"

Appearing, seemingly out of nowhere, this gentleman stood with one arm around his wife's shoulders and the other holding his daughter tightly. He also seemed to change as we observed him. As though time were moving through him, leaving him unaffected. The look on both of their faces was of contentment, a sense of peace and understanding. Surely, this is what we are all about. Beings, safe and secure in the environment we helped to create, stable and at peace with ourselves. If only we could bring this awareness to our physical world. Meredith and I looked at each other, recognizing the same accepted peace in ourselves. This was true reality.

"Ma petite choux. We are so very proud of you. You have grown into a lovely young woman as we have watched." We listened to this man speaking with a thick French accent, his look of pure love turning to one of concern. "We knew you would. But you must stop worrying about us. We are happily learning and growing and watching over you."

As Bree's father admonished her incessant mourning, Meredith and I observed her aura cleansing and changing to a solid blue tinged in golden yellow as though the sun were painting its rays into it and yielding bursts of violet color like scattered blossoms throughout the field that was her aura. This happened as energy from her father melted and blended itself into her energy. "That's fine, Papa," I thought to myself. "You've healed your daughter."

"The future is bright, Gabrielle. Have no fear. Your papa was a foolish man not to believe in the endless beauty of eternity. Those on Earth who love and care for you, those you have met recently, they have loved you through the ages, as we have. Trust in them and in their love for you. Let them guide you." Meredith and I looked at each other, puzzled, but somehow knowing he referred to us. "You are not alone. Always remember, nothing ever really dies, mon petite. We learn, we grow, we continue. Believe, Chu Chu. Believe."

The following morning, Meredith and I arrived simultaneously at Bree's doorstep, both obviously concerned for the possible aftershock of our apprentice. We laughed as we realized we shared the same thought, two silly geese looking out for the welfare of their gosling. Meredith spoke first. "I was concerned. She's had no previous experience with this type of phenomena."

Max answered the door and led us in, showing us to the library with a promise to announce our arrival and an offer of fresh coffee. Bree came in moments later. "I am so happy to see you both. Was that all just a dream, or was it real?"

She was fine, her aura intact. This was a new woman standing before us. Meredith and I smiled with relief.

"It was real, Bree. We both thought you might be having some difficulty with the experience. But you seem well!"

"Yes, Meredith, and I want to thank both of you. You know, when they hugged me, I could feel it. I could actually feel their arms around me. And they seemed so content. This has not only answered my questions, but given me something I thought I would never have again, time with my family." Her voice cracked a little and tears began to well in her eyes.

Meredith put her arm around Bree. "It's all right to feel emotional, Bree. This was an experience most do not have in their lives. But you are handling it very well. Consider it a reward for your spiritual progress."

"It was more than I could have hoped for. I wish people could know the truth about death; it would comfort them. For so many, fear permeates the misunderstandings they have. It could alleviate so much misery if people only knew. I honestly believe it would change so much for them even in their physical lifetime."

"Then I would say you have your work cut out for you. You have created a worthwhile mission for yourself. Is my assistant and gifted counselor ready for a full day at work?" Meredith's lighthearted tone was encouraging. The smile on Bree's face showed her appreciation. I thought about the statement Bree's father had made to her about the people in this realm who would love and guide her. I was absolutely certain he was referring to Meredith and me, but if we had a past life link, I was unaware of it. I filed the thought away in my subconscious to be considered another day. I didn't know it then, but that day would come soon.

There was a change in Bree after her encounter, a healed aura and a peace of mind not formerly apparent. I believed she was right. Many could benefit from the truth about the transformation we call death, and if Bree had anything to say about it, benefit they would.

# Chapter 5

I had never thought of children being a part of my life. My classrooms were filled with young adults, not children. My bachelor lifestyle was as comfortable to me as an old pair of slippers. I knew there were an abundant number of people needing the affirmation of childbirth, but I had never been one of them. Nevertheless, my personal fortune grew through encounters with children needing my help. The Angels fast became used to nightly departures as we continued our mission to return lost children. The memory of one we could have lost comes to mind as I choose the stories to relate to you.

Not long after our success with Annette, we realized we could possibly stop this sort of tragedy before it happened. We had been working with astral projection, and after drilling the difficult concept of the illusiveness of time and space, we began to work with the knowledge that time could be manipulated as easily as extending a thought. We discussed this subject in class one morning.

"Alex, with all the experiences you have had, surely the concept of the illusion of time and space cannot be this difficult for you."

"But Professor Evans, if what you are saying is true, we could go back and change history."

"How do you know someone hasn't?"

"Oh, good grief!"

"Why do you limit your imagination? Did Michelangelo paint with one color? You are a scientist with an artistic flair, not to mention experiences most would have difficulty imagining. Yet, for you, they are real. Why do you insist on limiting yourself?"

Early in our work of returning children, we had decided, as a group, that the less publicity the Angels had, the less restricted we would be in our endeavors. I realized I was treading dangerously close to the edge in opening this conversation in class. After all, the rest of my students were not aware of the Angels existence; and I was getting some very curious looks. I did a little damage control. "As all of you know, you are welcome to join us in meditation outside of class. Alex has benefited tremendously from this experience, as have the rest of the students who have chosen to take advantage of this opportunity." Since this extracurricular activity offered no extra credit, I was fairly safe in extending this offer.

"We have done some research into the manipulation of time and have experimented successfully in slowing it down and speeding it up. Alex has been a part of these experiments and naturally, I expect her to apply this knowledge and expand on it, as any good scientist would." This seemed to satisfy everyone's curiosity.

Later, at the New Age Counseling Center, they were all waiting for me, ready for one of our discussions.

"Really, Professor Evans, manipulating time?"

"Yes, Alex. I think we can use it in our work. I think we can intercept some abductions before they happen by manipulating time."

"I need an aspirin!"

"I'm serious, Alex. As we come to realize an abduction should never have happened, we could go back in time to where it began and alter the events."

"Even if we could do that, what would happen to the newspaper articles, the television broadcasts, and the flyer put out on that missing child?"

"They will have never existed."

"Of course." Mark looked inspired. "It's what you told us about the intricacies of time."

"Now you're thinking, Mark. Go on, explain to everyone."

"Don't you remember? We talked about the fact that there is more to time than just past, present, and future. Each tense has its own past, present, and future."

"And, if I may interrupt, by stepping into the past we can recreate its future. Hence the information on the missing child will disappear because the child won't be missing!"

An article with a photograph of Charles Brenton, age six, found its way into my hand. I looked up to see Meredith slowly drawing away after placing it there.

"Is he next, Meredith?"

# Chapter 6

Charles Brenton was abducted by his own father, a misguided drug addict looking for someone to blame for his own misery. His wife Eleanor, according to the article in the New York Herald; had left him after his last failure at drug rehabilitation. After all, she had Charles to protect and life with an addicted parent was no life at all. Eleanor knew this. If it wasn't for Charles, she would have ended her own life. Living with Jeff was nothing more than living a nightmare. She never knew what kind of abuse she was in for when this man would walk through the door. He had struck her many times, in rages brought on by cocaine, alcohol, and lack of funds to support both habits. To this point, she had managed to keep Charles away from this madness, but she knew it was only a matter of time before he saw his mom being beaten by his dad; before he himself might be victimized by his own father. She knew she had to get him away from this environment. So one night, after Jeff had passed out from too much bourbon, she packed the car, strapped her sleeping little boy into the passenger seat, and drove all night. In Larkspur, New Jersey, she woke her parents. They were safe. She thought they were safe.

Eleanor awoke in her old bedroom. As she slowly returned to consciousness, she was mentally transported back to her high school days when she lived in this house, when she lived without fear. Charles slept peacefully in the twin bed next to hers. Her father had bought the bed years ago for her friends to use when they spent the night. Now it held her sleeping son. She had done the right thing. After his all night ride, Charles was exhausted. Good, it would give her enough time to come up with a plausible explanation about why they had to visit Grandma and Grandpa, and why Daddy couldn't come along. Eleanor became aware of the aromatic scent of freshly brewing coffee. She got up, selected a robe from the closet, and went downstairs to join her mother.

"Is Charles still sleeping, Dear?"

"Yes, Mom. I think he will sleep for a while. What will I tell him? I don't want him traumatized by all of this."

"I don't know, Ell; but whatever you come up with will be better than what you have saved him from experiencing. Why didn't you confide in me about Jeff sooner?"

"I thought, or hoped, it would all change; that he would see he couldn't go on like this and benefit from his rehab. If not for me, for Charlie." Eleanor, nearly in tears, accepted consolation and a cup of hot coffee from her mother.

"Dad left for his office early this morning, but he said to tell you that this has always been your home and it always will be. You take some time and rest. We can raid the Christmas closet and give Charlie a few toys early this year. That and a batch of double fudge brownies should keep him busy enough that he won't ask questions, at least for today."

"Mom, you're the greatest."

When Charlie finally opened his eyes, it was after noon. Like any six year old, he reacted to his strange surroundings with fear.

"Mom!"

"It's O.K., Sweetie. We're at Grandma's."

"Why, Mom?"

"Well, Charles, Grandma has a lot of surprises for you. She missed you so much, I decided to drive you down so you could visit. Maybe we will stay here for a while. You would like to stay, wouldn't you, Charlie?"

"I guess. Will Daddy be staying, too?"

"No, Baby, not this trip. Aren't you hungry?"

Eleanor led her son down to the kitchen for lunch and one of Grandma's homemade brownies. Her mom was right, brownies can make all the difference. It did almost seem like Christmas to watch Charles discover his new toys with the kind of wide-eyed excitement only a child displays. He selected a few and requested that he be able to play in the yard. Eleanor felt relieved at not having to explain further, and as she watched her son walk out the door, she turned and hugged her mother.

It was a beautiful spring day, blue sky, fluffy white clouds, crisp clean air. The yard made a perfect playground for Charles and he happily took advantage of it. Charles was also delighted when he saw his father's car turn the corner and stop at the gate to the yard.

Charles did not see us. The Angels managed to stay out of his sight, and wait . . . wait for what? This was becoming a tense situation. We knew by Charlie's reaction that his father was beginning the drama that was unfolded for us in the previous day's newspaper.

"Chuck."

"Daddy!" The little boy, understandably happy to see his father and unaware of any danger, ran to his open arms.

"Mom will be happy you're here."

"Yes, Son. Let's go first and buy her some flowers, all right?"

As easily as that, Charlie was gone in his father's car. His father, of course, had no intention of returning him.

"I don't know how, but we have to find a way to stay with them." I had little experience tailing people, especially in an astral form. Meredith, however, had her own ideas.

"Envision Charlie and his father. As we do that, we will be at their destination." With that thought expressed, we were transported.

"Good Lord, where are we?"

"I don't know, Mark, but this is no environment for a little boy." People unconscious or semiconscious, lay around this place. "They're drugged. This is some sort of drug house. He can't possibly be bringing that little boy here!" Meredith's tone turned to one of complete disgust.

We heard the front door open. Charles, in the company of his father, walked timidly through the door. "I don't think we will find flowers here, Daddy."

"No Son, no flowers. We're going to play a little trick on Mommy, like the one she played on me; you know, when she drove off last night."

This man had no heart. He had no soul. How could he bring a child, any child, to a place like this, let alone his own son? Charlie started to react to the fear welling inside of him.

"Look, you'll be just fine. Be my big boy; you're a brave boy, right? Daddy has to get some cigarettes. You wait here. I'll be right back."

"Please, Daddy, don't leave me here!" The child was on the verge of hysterics. It was unbearable to watch. But we could not interfere in his conversation with his father. We had to wait for the father to leave. That would be our opportunity to resolve this situation. A sense of danger became overwhelming. As a group, we began meditating to get the energy working for us.

"Now stop whining. I said I'd be right back. You sit over there and I'll bring you back a surprise. But only if you behave."

With that, he turned and walked out the door, leaving a trembling child in the corner. The sight of Charlie, feeling his fear and abandonment, was almost too much to bear.

"Charlie." Meredith spoke with the intonation of a child calling another to play. "Charlie, over here. Come see what I have for you." The little boy dried his tears with his sleeve and turned to see six smiling faces. "We found those flowers for your mom. Let's go take them to her."

Bree started to lose control. She looked as though she would break down in tears. I put my arm around her waist, a gesture to bolster her spirit. "We have to maintain a cheerful attitude here, Bree." She responded with the courage I had come to expect from her.

"Charlie, what's your mom's favorite color?"

"Yellow."

"Good, we have yellow tulips. Let's go"

"But my dad told me to stay and wait for him. I'm not supposed to talk to strangers."

"That's right, Charlie, but this is the one exception you must make. You can't stay here. This isn't a good place. You know that, don't you?" Mark sounded convincing, appealing to the child's growing sense of danger. "We will get you back to your toys in your grandma's yard. You'd rather be there, right?"

As confused and frightened as he was, he knew instinctively that he didn't want to wait in this horrible place. From behind her back, Meredith creatively produced a bunch of sunny yellow tulips.

"Are you angels?"

We had become used to that question. It was an easy explanation. Alex had the routine down. "That's right, Charlie. We're going to help you. We get sent to Earth to help little boys just like you."

He walked over and nestled among us like a yearling recognizing safety among his own kind. We got him outside, down several blocks, and back to his grandparents' yard. In this quiet place, we sat him down at the picnic table. Meredith began to talk to Charlie in a soothing repetitive manner. She was hypnotizing him and he was responding. As his eyes started to close, she told him that the house he saw was only in a bad dream. Like any bad dream, it was best forgotten. We waited, watching Charlie sleep, not wanting to leave his side until we were certain he was safe. Finally, Eleanor came outside to find Charlie sound asleep at the picnic table, clutching a bunch of yellow tulips.

"Where in the world did he get these?" she wondered out loud. She picked him up and carried him in for his nap.

We have all had the experience of doing something and not really knowing why until it was over and we could see retrospectively. We would use time manipulation again; but not frequently. In this instance, we were soon to be made aware of why it had become necessary:

### EXPLOSION IN DRUG HOUSE IN LARKSPUR, NEW JERSEY

Among the ten bodies found at this residence, a native of New York City, Jeffrey L. Brenton, dead at age 32.

After reading this article, we all became silent, in awe of the opportunity to save a life, in awe of the way it played out. Had we not been able to return Charlie to his grandparents' home, reversing events, he would have been the eleventh victim in that drug house explosion.

# Chapter 7

S ummer had flown and before I knew it I was beginning my second year at Fields University. My students seemed glued to this class. There was a waiting list of eager people interested in parapsychology. We talked of expanding the department because of its immense popularity. I approached this year with fresh ideas to make the class as interesting and fulfilling as possible. We were looking forward to a year filled with fascinating guest speakers, unusual experimentation, and an agenda that flowed as magically as its subject. I couldn't be happier in my new home or my new place of employment where I was surrounded by wonderful friends. The Angels had continued through the summer in search of lost children. With the help of Meredith who, with inspiration, lead our searches, we had returned twenty-four children. With all my experience teaching, nothing could compare with the rush of finding missing children and leading them home before anyone was able to harm them, or in some cases, as that of Charles, even to miss them. I look back fondly on memories of Annette and Charles, as well as many others, wondering what the future would have been like without them. Did we save a future president who would unite the world in peace? Did we return a child who would grow up to find the missing element in the cure to all incurable diseases? Did we return the future grandmother who would give more love to her grandchildren than most could fathom? And in so doing, would one of her own grow up to realize and implement the dreams of Martin Luther King, Jr.? It was an awesome subject to think about. Humans had so much inherent possibility. Missing even one could potentially upset the balance of so many lives. And I was especially proud of the Angels. I was proud of their stamina in pursuing missing kids, their ability to keep private all of the marvelous things they had accomplished in order to focus all of their energy on our most precious objective. As young as these people were, there wasn't an ego among them feeling the need to announce to anyone what they had learned and achieved in order to receive praise and adulation. Our reward was in the contemplation of the joy we were able to help produce by returning loved ones to their families.

Yes, Meredith was right. Calvert was where I belonged, and Calvert was where I would stay.

The return of autumn reminded me of my first introduction to this little town. I wondered at how unexpectedly I was brought here and at how, in one short year my life had flourished beyond any previous expectation. Bree, after her reunion with her parents, blossomed and became Meredith's right hand. We fell into our respective places like so many puzzle pieces. And the picture we created as a whole, including all of the Angels, in my opinion was rivaled by none. Commitment and accomplishment, what human could ask for more to fulfill their lives?

As she was so accustomed to doing, Meredith dropped by the Saturday before the first day of class.

"So what is first on your agenda for the new year, Professor?"

"Well, Meredith, I've been thinking. Bree has mentioned many times her interest in exploring reincarnation. I can't help but feel there is some sort of connection between her interest and our endeavors. However, we must put that off for now. There is an urgent need. Our help has been sought in rooting out the source of a problem in the old Jameson estate not far from the university campus. Have you heard anything about this?"

"Yes, it seems there are several unexplained disturbances in that mansion."

"That's an understatement! I will fill you in, but I was wondering if you would be interested in trying to communicate with these entities, if in fact that is what we are dealing with. Help me try to solve this problem?"

"I would be happy to, Lang. It disturbs me that spirits can be so out of sync with their own environment that they remain long after their physical bodies have gone. I am always glad for a chance to assist them."

"Good, I thought I could count on you. If you could make it to my first class with us Monday morning, we will make some plans to attend our ghostly manifestations. I wanted to use this opportunity as a learning situation for the students. We can't take them all with us, of course, but we can take a group; and they will report back to the rest on their experience."

"Bree called this morning and asked if we had plans for dinner."

"Dinner at the Victorian mansion with Bree? How could I resist?"

We had been dining regularly together since my arrival in Calvert. It was amazing how well good friends and wholesome food could inspire this old professor. I always looked forward to feasting and sharing conversations with Bree and Meredith. "I'll bring the wine."

At dinner that evening we discussed the request I had informed Meredith about earlier. Bree showed quite a bit of interest in attending.

"I don't see why not, Bree. You certainly have had experience with discarnates. I think your attendance and your meditative ability would be most helpful."

I whimsically thought to myself that Bree was no longer the timid young woman who would have had a heart attack in a dark room facing an unknown entity. How far she had come. How far she would still progress.

"Wonderful. What's happening in that old house?" Bree was ready to get to work.

Although they had heard there was a problem, neither Bree nor Meredith had been filled in on the details of the haunting that was evidently going on in the residence of Doctor and Mrs. Jameson. I had taken a call a few days before from an unusual source. Reverend Anderson, minister of the Calvert Methodist Church, phoned requesting a meeting with me. Doctor and Mrs. Jameson were members of his parish and had come to him with bizarre details of unnerving experiences in their home. At a loss as to how to handle the situation, Reverend Anderson remembered the class his son Joe insisted on taking at the university. The class was in parapsychology. Joe had been an interested student and delved into many psychic subjects with enthusiasm, although most were contrary to his father's beliefs and definitely without his approval. But as Reverend Anderson knew well, his son must find his own path, and he encouraged him to approach all things with an open mind. It seemed that his son's decision to pursue parapsychology inspired Reverend Anderson to phone me when his attempt to rid the Jameson house of unwanted house guests through prayer had failed. In fact, prayer seemed to make the unwanted guests even more spirited, if you will excuse the pun, and infinitely more turbulent in their attempt to disconcert the Jameson household. It was as though the prayer for their benefit reassured them that they were making themselves known. Since that was their apparent intention, why stop? From odd noises and doors being opened, seemingly under their own power, the manifestations had advanced to dishes flying through the air, only to land with a resounding crash in pieces on the kitchen floor. Razor blades were dangerously inspired to flight in similar situations in Dr. Jameson's bath. Reading and listening to music became distressing diversions as the Jameson's were frequently treated to resounding marching band music, replacing their soothing Debussy and Mozart selections. And often at these times, normally undisturbed artifacts, positioned securely on sturdy shelves, crashed to the floor with no apparent reason for their sudden descent.

The phone became a dreaded interruption. Upon answering, the Jameson's were often treated to the sounds of miserable, wretched moaning, and heart-stopping screams. Having heard the antics of these apparitions, I was unsure that, with all my experience, I could tolerate these demonstrations without coming to my wits end. My heart went out to the Jameson's, when I realized how dramatically their peaceful lives were being interrupted. After all, Dr. Jameson was a respected retired physician. Surely, there was no preparation in either of their lives for such encounters. The library of the old mansion could no longer be used safely. Doctor Jameson was especially annoyed that the spirits had chosen that room in which to wreak havoc, since that was the room of which he was most fond. But it became obvious in passing weeks, since Reverend Anderson's well-intentioned prayer sessions, that one could come to serious bodily harm by remaining for any length of time in the library. In that room, objects and furniture would not only find their imaginary wings, but would often be propelled in the direction of the head of the unwanted human intruder who dared to enter. Either the spirits would have to be encouraged to leave, or the Jamesons would have to move from their beloved home.

The mansion was inherited quite unexpectedly by Doctor Jameson, he being the sole survivor of the Jameson family. It was originally owned by Philip T. Jameson. Upon his sudden and unexpected death, the house remained unoccupied for many years until Doctor Jameson was found in the state of Illinois. Doctor and Mrs. Jameson moved to Wisconsin after being informed of their inheritance and the deed was transferred, with little ceremony, to the last of the Jameson clan. Both Doctor Jameson and his wife had resided in the house comfortably for thirty years. Why, at this time, should these occurrences commence? That was a question that required too much detail to answer during a phone conversation, but I had assured the Reverend that such time lapses were not unusual.

I had hope of bringing Meredith into the house, especially the library, and through her sensitivity, determine the nature of this unrest, as well as who the perpetrators were. Then, as is often the case, we could settle whatever dispute or misunderstanding, explain alternate possibilities to our unseen guests, and they would leave the residence in peace. At least, that was what we hoped for.

Bree seemed amused with the Jamesons' dilemma. "I don't mean to take this lightly. I'm sure the Jamesons are beside themselves; but I can't help but see the humor in this. These apparitions sound like naughty two year olds trying to get attention."

Meredith tried, in vain, to stifle a grin. "That does present a humorous picture, Bree. Of course, spirits do not belong in a physical world. When they feel they are unable to leave, their frustration at not being able to communicate, coupled with their inability to move into a more compatible environment, causes them to become mischievous and sometimes destructive. The psyche is prone to all sorts of self-inflicted dilemmas, whether in the physical realm or not." As earnest as this explanation was, Meredith was infected with the humor Bree saw in the situation. The two laughed imagining some of these foolish antics.

"I can't believe you two are amused at the misery that has befallen the Jamesons." Meredith and Bree looked at each other, then at me, and once again started to laugh hysterically. I guess it was rather funny. "O.K., you've had your levity for the day. Now take this seriously, both of you; these people could be physically harmed or even scared to death. They're not young, you know."

"You're right, Lang, of course. It's no laughing matter. It's just that Bree's interpretation of the antics of two year olds struck me as amusing. And really, they do take on the qualities of naughty children. But of course, this is a serious situation. I will do all I can to help."

"Me, too." Trying to compose themselves, Bree and Meredith became overly serious.

"You may not be this delighted stuck in a haunted house. We will see who has the last laugh."

Monday morning arrived and with it, the first of my classes for the first day of the new semester. After settling in, we discussed the problem at the Jameson mansion. I explained that I would be taking a total of ten volunteers, two from each of my classes, with me on our assignment. The Angels would, of course, accompany me as well. Their work in astral projection honed their psychic skills beyond the awareness of the rest of my students. Their help using focused meditative expertise would be invaluable support to

Meredith as she "tuned in" to the world of spirit. Throughout the day, I had more volunteers than I could handle, and chose, at random for the most part, the ten who would become personally involved in the de-haunting of the Jameson place. I explained to them that it would be necessary for them to keep accurate notes on what transpired in the home, as they would have the task of reporting the proceedings to each of their respective classes.

The day chosen was the following Saturday. We chose this day because we didn't know how long we would be at the house. It was not unusual to spend an entire day and remain throughout the night to entice the spirits to make themselves known to strangers. After all, their usual diversification was lavished on the residents only. Intruders were often ignored and the festivities would not begin until after their departure. It was then necessary to convince the spirits that we would remain until such a time when they chose to make themselves known to us. With encouragement from Meredith, hovering between both worlds, we would hopefully peak their interest enough that they would respond to her. The usual electronic equipment was set in place; cameras with infrared film to catch any unusual movement and devices that measured everything from temperature changes to the slightest motion. But our greatest awareness came from a human source. Although nothing unusual happened at first, Meredith immediately sensed their presence. After a group meditation, Meredith, without knowing where the room was, walked directly to the library. There she continued her meditation and gently chanted over and over, inviting communication from the spirits locked in the house.

I had sent Alex to the Calvert Historical Society to look up the history of the Jameson estate. She joined us with valuable and colorful information. Alex had discovered that Philip T. Jameson lived a bachelor's life in the late nineteenth century. He was an affluent attorney in his time and attracted many of the opposite sex. It seems that Barrister Jameson had committed the irrevocable sin of courting many of the town's finest eligible maidens, hence promising marriage to not one, but all. In fact, he either chose to remain a bachelor, or his life was terminated at the tender age of thirty-four, before he could render his decision. His conquests had apparently discovered each other. What was never pursued was the possibility that Barrister Jameson, who died quite suddenly of an apparent bout of influenza, may have in actuality been poisoned by one or more of his intended. This came to no more than speculation and in turn, colorful folklore on the part of local citizens. Since the nearest physician and coroner were several hundred miles from Calvert, Philip was interred before any questions arose.

Having read this bit of information, Meredith logically concluded that Philip had not come to terms with his unexpected demise, however manifested. Surely he remained in the house. The question was, was he alone? Meredith's instinctive response to this was that there was more than one spirit locked in this house. Amy looked puzzled. "But why start haunting now? I mean, all of this happened one hundred years ago!"

Doctor and Mrs. Jameson joined the group. "That's what we would like to know." Dr. Jameson's tone was impatient. A man of considerable size, he looked as though he had not slept and, of course, that was the case. Mrs. Jameson was a petite, white-haired woman, with a pink-and-white complexion. She looked to be a gentle, shy individual. But it was apparent that she suffered from these unwanted intrusions, as well.

I greeted the couple. "This will take some time, Doctor. Why don't we discuss this in the living room. I will answer all of your questions and explain our plans."

The living room of the Jameson mansion was made up of

ornately carved Louis XV French court walnut furniture. My students seemed reluctant to sit down on the embossed satin fabric. Several chairs and three couches were grouped around an immense lavishly carved Italian marble fireplace. An imposing oil portrait of a handsome man, dressed impeccably in a Victorian waistcoat, hung on the wall above the fireplace. The room was large enough to accommodate everyone.

"Please, make yourselves comfortable." Mrs. Jameson admonished, noticing the students' hesitation. "I will ring for tea."

After everyone was seated and tea had been served, I attempted to explain to this bewildered couple what was happening in their home. I felt especially sorry for them. My own parents, in the medical profession themselves, would also have been at a loss to deal with this situation. After all, it was outside the realm of anything they had experienced. Pondering the dilemma of the Jamesons, I finally understood why my parents had been unable to accept my abilities and my chosen profession. Of course, just as the Jamesons, they had no frame of reference, no experience with such phenomena. But unlike my parents, the Jamesons were about to be inducted through a crash course in parapsychology. They had no choice. The spirit world had invaded their home, and they were caught in the middle of the invasion.

"We are dealing with spirits who have passed on, no longer housed in physical form; but for some reason, they have not accepted their transition. Amy, you have asked, as have many of you, why these apparitions are causing all this havoc now, after so much time has passed. You need to understand that time is something we are subjected to; however, those in spirit do not experience time in the same way we do. They are not controlled by it. They do not see change in themselves due to time. They could sleep for one hundred years or more without being aware that such a span of time had passed."

I was about to begin an explanation of our plan to find and ultimately release the spirits when I noticed Meredith looking as though she were in trance. "Meredith?"

"Philip is here, Lang. That is his portrait, isn't it?" She did not wait for an answer. "And three female spirits. I sense an Amanda, Clarise, and Josette." At this declaration, as if in response, a vase on the fireplace mantle fell with a resounding crash, scattering cut flowers, water, and broken crystal across the marble floor surrounding the fireplace. The students collectively caught their breath.

"Don't be alarmed. They're just acknowledging Meredith's recognition." It seemed this day would see many frayed nerves.

"Philip was murdered, poisoned. He is very angry at having his perfect life ended so abruptly, so violently." Meredith sounded emotional and tears began to well in her eyes.

"Don't share his pain, Meredith. Not now. That won't help. We need you to remain in control. Stabilize yourself, for heaven's sake; stay with us!" Meredith was slipping into Philp's emotions, feeling his anguish over his fate. I had to encourage her to remain focused. She took a deep breath, regained her composure, and went on.

"He feels quite sorry for himself. You were correct, Lang. After the shock of his passing, he did fall into a deep sleep. This man apparently was under the impression that after death there was nothing, so he basically slept until he could no longer deny his own awareness. Of course, by that time, the women who administered the poison had also met with their own ends. It is their reaction to his anger which keeps them here, as well. This man is far, far too angry. I have to walk."

With that declaration, Meredith got up and started walking, again toward the library. I was right behind her, followed by Bree, Doctor and Mrs. Jameson, and the students. Meredith opened the library door.

"Oh, my God!" Mark's reaction to what he saw in the library summed up our astonishment as a group. In place of Dr. Jameson's massive mahogany desk, a chaise lounge rested. Eerily visible, but without true substance, it stood in the center of the room. Philip lay on it, seemingly unaware of any other presence, sound asleep.

Through the French doors that separated the library from the hall, three female spirits cautiously approached so as not to awaken their sleeping victim. A cloth, possibly soaked in chloroform or ether, was held over Philip's nose and mouth as two of the female spirits held him down. He seemed to awaken briefly to protest, but quickly succumbed to the effects. Next, one of them produced a goblet filled with a burgundy-colored liquid that she forced into Philip's mouth and massaged down his throat. We stepped aside as the spirits lifted Philip off the chaise lounge and proceeded to carry him, with apparent difficulty, up the stairs. We followed them to the master bedroom, where they lay Philip down on his bed. All of this was visible to us through the energy and constancy of Meredith's connection between both worlds. As the spirits vanished, I caught Meredith who, losing her balance, fell back in exhaustion. Then hearing sounds from the hall, we turned to find that the women had reappeared. Horrified at what they had done, they held on to each other and sobbed. One was turned enough for us to notice, despite her flowing Victorian skirts, that she was with child. Of the three, she sobbed the most, pitifully hysterical. Finally, they helped each other descend the stairs, and halfway down they vanished again.

We were speechless at the scene we had witnessed. Meredith, regaining her composure, started first down the steps and began calling to Philip. "You must end this now, Philip. You must not stay here. Foolishness! Replaying the events of your death and trying to reclaim your life and your house! Release these women. It's over. The time to move on has long since passed."

Clearly, Philip was not happy with this idea. Breaking loose from everywhere, anything movable took flight. My instinct was to protect the Jamesons from objects hurling through the open staircase. The rest of us could take care of ourselves. I turned to instruct them to sit down on the stairs where they would be surrounded and protected by the rest of us. As I did, I caught a plant at the back of my head.

"Lang!" For the first time since this incredible scene began, Meredith lost her composure.

"Don't worry, I'm not hurt."

Satisfied with my response, Meredith reached into a pocket and produced a white candle. She lit the candle, which immediately seemed to snuff its own flame. Undaunted, she lit the candle again and started down the steps ahead of us.

As she walked, she spoke to the spirits. "You must follow me. You have replayed this scene enough. You are doomed to repeat it for eternity only because of your own foolish insistence. Follow the light and get on with your existence. You will have other lifetimes in which to work out your problems. Philip, Josette, Clarisse, Amanda. Follow me. It's time. It's for the best."

The rest of us, helpless to assist, watched as Meredith, holding the candle before her, led what seemed to be energized glittering gusts of wind out the door.

"It is done." I helped Doctor and Mrs. Jameson to their feet. "They won't be back."

# Chapter 8

On Monday morning, the news of the haunting of the Jameson mansion was all anyone in the entire school was talking about. My classes were filled to capacity with curious students, many of whom were there only because of all the rumors they had heard. Many had never considered taking a class in parapsychology, but they could not resist the temptation of hearing about the events that happened on the previous Saturday.

Mark, in my first class of the day, asked about the Jamesons. "Did it work, Professor? Are the spirits going to leave them alone?"

"As far as we know, there is no more disturbance in the mansion. Of course, it has been less than two days. Whether or not they return is something we will have to wait to see. I know of no one who will guarantee that a ghost will not stubbornly return to his haunting. Hopefully, Meredith convinced them of the futility of their endeavors."

"What makes a spirit decide to haunt a house?" I knew questions like this one would prevail at least for the rest of the day, if not longer. So today's lessons would deal with life after death. Certainly a worthwhile area of study which affects us all.

"First, we need to examine spirit and determine what type it is."

"There's more than one?"

"There are two, Louis. In class, we have studied auras, a name given to the electrical energy emitted by and surrounding living beings. As we live and think and respond in life, that energy is sent forth and often soaks into the very walls of the dwellings which we consistently inhabit."

"So the energy of the residents in a building sticks around after they are gone?"

"That's right, Joe. Sort of like fingerprints. In old buildings, especially, having accumulated so much energy and filled to capacity, it will burst out, energy will be released, and manifestations will be seen. But these manifestations are not true spirit. They are imprints of the past. You might see what seems to be the spirit of a woman, moving as though she were climbing a staircase which is not there. On old blueprints of the house, you may find that the original house had such a staircase, which was then removed for remodeling. The spirit is actually nothing more than an imprint of something this woman may have done hundreds of times long ago.

Then again, as in the case of the Jameson mansion, people may find, after their physical demise, that they do not wish to leave that which is familiar to them. Or they may be so confused about death that all they focus on and ultimately all they see is what they have left behind, and they imprison themselves in an environment that no longer responds to them. Without a physical body, we cannot function in a physical world. Some find it too frightening or confusing to venture on and so they stay. Imagine how you would feel if one day you woke up at home only to find that no one in your house could hear or see you. You would try everything you could think of to communicate with the people in your house. Failing that, you would become despondent and bitter. That is the type of personality one must deal with in releasing spirits. Often, due to lack of training in the nature of their own spirituality, or ties because of unexpected circumstance, spirits lock themselves into their physical environment and can spend years, sometimes centuries, bemoaning their fate. As in the case of Philip Jameson, one could fall victim to an abrupt end, sleep for long periods of time as we know it, and finally awaken to a nightmare replayed over and over, like a bad dream that cannot be dismissed, a dream of their own creation. It is a sad situation, and one that could prove deadly to those of us being subjected to it."

"Deadly? You mean they could harm someone?"

"That's right, Kate. As all of the students who accompanied us will attest to, the Jameson house was a dangerous place to be on Saturday. Obviously, objects being hurled at one could cause serious harm, not to mention the possibility of a person unfamiliar with what he is experiencing being scared to death. You must also remember that these spirits are no different from you or me. They have fears and respond to situations seemingly out of their control as all of us would. Locked into such a nightmare, they become destructive to the point of being described as evil. Fortunately, the Jameson case was dealt with before these manifestations got worse."

"It could have been worse?" Amy was clearly taken aback with this realization.

"There have been cases of spirits starting fires, attacking children, and causing such ghastly phenomenon as to drive residents from their homes in fear. That is if they were fortunate enough to escape. This is serious business, Ladies and Gentlemen. Caution must always be exercised in dealing with beings who believe they have nothing to lose, regardless of what plane they reside in."

"How do these things happen, Professor Evans? How do spirits come to haunt a house?"

"It's not as unusual as you might think, Alex. The human psyche is subject to all kinds of self-inflicted illusions, especially out of body, until they understand they are controlling their environment."

"What do you mean by 'especially out of body'?"

"When you are no longer in a physical state, the true creator, pure thought creates instantly. Imagine how your own thoughts instantly transferred into reality could affect you."

"Anything I thought, even a passing fear instantly would be real?"

"That's right, Mark. Just as you have to adjust to new situations here, a being having passed into the next life must understand his new environment. Someone without training or belief in an afterlife could become very confused. Of course, they would not understand that their situation was under their control.

They would respond out of fear that would bring more fearful conditions. As we have discussed in studying astral projection, it is necessary, once you are out of body, to think of where you want to be. Keeping clear thoughts and objectives will keep your mind from wandering thereby creating unattractive situations. That's why I feel it is so important for us to understand the great extent to which we create our worlds. That knowledge prepares us for ultimately living in a world where all things are created through direct thought energy. If a person dies with no training in what to expect at death, that person may go into a deep sleep. To him, this sleep simulates death. But, as we all do, eventually he will awaken. But awaken to find what? He had no expectation of life after death. Since he feels no less alive than he did before his death, all that he knows to be real is the world he left behind. And so, once again awake, he focuses his attention on the physical world. He sees nothing else because he believes nothing else exists. His desires are only with the physical and he wishes to see nothing else. He knows he is alive and he needs to communicate that to someone. But everyone he approaches seems not to notice him, or worse, to ignore him. And so he returns to his home or some other familiar place and the cycle begins."

"But he is in spirit. Why doesn't he see the world of spirit and go there?"

"As I said, he does not believe it exists, and therefore masks its presence, seeing only the physical world he can no longer function in. His frustration mounting, he tries whatever he can think of to bring attention to himself. Do you see the direction this is going in?"

"A frightening one!" shuddered Mark.

"Unfortunate and frightening, Mark. But that is not the only scenario of the trapped spirit. The one, who in life believed in life after death, but at death had not yet vanquished the physical and psychological cravings of addiction. This spirit would want to relive his addictions to alcohol or drugs. He would seek only those still in physical bodies who, like him, were caught in this destructive behavior. By blending his spirit with the auras of those abusing their preferred substance, the spirit can experience the high to which he was a slave while in his physical body. This process keeps him from acknowledging further existence, and keeps the one whose aura he is attached to encouraged to continue abuse. This is another sad and vicious cycle. We do all we can, but we must remember that nothing ever really dies. Eventually even the most pitiable spirit will tire of his conditions and ask for help. Then his world will open to him, and those who have been waiting patiently to reach him will appear miraculously to guide him. They come seemingly from out of nowhere, and yet they have been there for him throughout the entire process. All that was needed was his acceptance and his request for help."

Louis, ever perplexed by philosophies, entered into the conversation. "Some religions teach that when we die, we sleep until we are summoned with the return of the Messiah."

"Louis, regardless of what religion you are accustomed to, know this: When you leave this physical plane, expect to see something. Expect to feel as alive as you ever have, possibly more so. The speculation of religions and redemption is all well and good, but do not let those theories color or limit your options to the point where you block attempts to help you. Religions are good for nourishing our spirit and teaching us to live morally in a physical world. But understand that you must learn to navigate your own environment, wherever that environment is. Stay open-minded, joyful, and interested in this life as well as the next. Then someone won't have the task of removing your spirit from a dreaded haunting! I am forever being caught in the "them-versus-us" attitude people adopt having been brought up in one or another religion. Religion is a speculative concept. Some are controlling. Your choice of worship, should you choose such a path, is a personal decision; however, any religion that appears to control through fear and disallows your own personal growth is one you should reconsider. Our spirituality is something that is a great part of each of us. Without it, we would not be here; we would not exist at all. Understanding and experiencing this life and the ones to follow, through growing spiritual awareness, is the greatest measure of growth and freedom that we can allow for ourselves. Knowing yourselves, who you are, what you are capable of achieving, is the greatest thing you can do for yourselves. No one has the right to interrupt that process of evolution, and the only way they can is if you allow it."

Mounting interest was overwhelming. Many people were trying to get information on the haunting. I was quietly amused at the response. As much as some choose to debunk and ignore the psychic world, its attraction is naturally found in the depths of each soul. Meredith joined me for lunch and, relying on our friendship, I enlisted her help for the rest of the afternoon. I had done so much talking all morning that my voice was deserting me. Having her in class to answer questions gave me a rest. I also enjoyed the opportunity to observe her good nature, her patience, and her enthusiasm while bringing truth to as many as would listen. And that day, thanks to the Jameson ghosts, there were many listening.

"The psychic world will never ask you to accept any concept on faith, Joe." Joe Anderson felt attached to the whole experience. His father, Reverend Anderson, would not have contacted me during his search to help the Jamesons had Joe not encouraged him. Meredith was gently answering Joe's questions and encouraging his curiosity. "Faith is a wonderful trait and works well in many situations. But true knowledge comes from experience, understanding, and practice. With these ideals, coupled with a desire to learn and grow, you cannot help becoming in tune, illumined, aware. The knowledge is not handed to you, however. You must want it and then work to achieve it, just as you would with anything worthwhile."

As I was listening to Meredith, and knowing my class was in capable hands, I began to think back. Meredith, as much as anyone I had met so far in this lifetime, had certainly attained spirituality through rigorous applied and often stubborn will. Born to a family where psychic ability was as real as any accepted truth, she was encouraged from a very early age to tune in to her true nature. She displayed enviable psychic talents even as a young child. Her encouragement at home was not mirrored in school, however; and there she met with serious opposition to the way she viewed the world.

A story she had told me about an experience in the fifth grade popped into my head. I tried to imagine a young Meredith as she explained how she knew upcoming events in advance of their happening. In the middle of delivering a book report on Moby Dick, she casually glanced over at her teacher and immediately lost her train of thought. Encouraged to continue, she began to stutter, then described personal belongings of the teacher. She told her she saw her driving a blue car, wearing shorts and a tee shirt and baseball cap, her hair tucked into the cap, and heading for the dock. There she saw her boarding a large fishing boat. She encouraged her teacher to make sure extra water and safety equipment was on board before she left on her excursion. A bewildered teacher told Meredith to go to the nurse's office and lie down for the rest of the morning.

Meredith was not surprised when, three days later, on a Sunday morning, her fifth-grade teacher phoned her home. The teacher explained to Meredith's mother that, having remembered what Meredith had told her, she automatically checked the water supply and safety equipment. She found there was not enough water and the safety equipment was not packed. After pointing this out to the owner of the boat, the problem was remedied, yet she was still apprehensive about boarding. An hour later, unexpectedly on a choppy, stormy ocean, the fishing expedition found themselves in the middle of nowhere. Nothing visible could be used to guide the vessel to safety. They needed to wait out the storm. Without the extra water and equipment, they could have been in serious trouble.

Meredith's abilities became well known at an early age. Some of the children, probably out of jealousy or fear, teased the girl until she had virtually introverted herself. Her parents, however, reassured her whenever possible and reminded her of what a valuable and sensitive gift she had. "You will do wondrous things with this ability." they repeatedly told her. "You will help people in ways most could not fathom." Without their support, young Meredith would no doubt have become sullen and reclusive, as this child's level of sensitivity was quite high. But, as only the strength of a loving family can nurture and guide one through one's lessons, with their caring assistance, she flourished. Surely those who knew Meredith and were infinitely helped through her talent, owed a debt of gratitude to the family that produced and carefully molded the woman who stood before me.

As I sat and listened and daydreamed, a messenger entered the classroom and handed me a note from the office. The Jamesons phoned the office to extend an invitation to Meredith, Bree, and me. Dinner at the Jamesons was on the agenda for that night. Surely Bree and Meredith would be delighted.

We arrived at the Jameson mansion and were greeted by Mrs. Jameson. She looked rested and lovely, a beneficial change from the frightened timid woman I had met on the previous Saturday. In fact, the mansion itself seemed somehow a different place. It was a welcome happy home as opposed to the haunted fragmented building so desperately in need of relief from its unwanted guests.

"Thank you all for coming on such short notice. Dr. Jameson and I wanted an opportunity to talk with you and tell you how grateful we are for all of your help."

Mrs. Jameson led us into the living room where Dr. Jameson was waiting. He stood as we entered the room.

"Professor Evans, Meredith, Bree, please make yourselves at home."

Dr. Jameson also looked refreshed. He was smiling as I reached to shake his hand. "It is good to see both of you in such fine spirits, Dr. Jameson."

"Thanks to all of you and your students. Alice and I were at our wits' end. I don't know what would have become of us without your help."

"The cook has laid out the table; why don't we go into the dining room. He becomes very agitated if we let his dinner get cold!" Mrs. Jameson took us to the dining room, the table laden with several wonderful dishes.

"We planned the evening's menu with several vegetarian dishes for you. We hope you will enjoy them." Mrs. Jameson smiled warmly.

"Everything looks delicious." I said as Dr. Jameson seated me at the head of the table.

"I'm curious, Professor. What became of our unseen guests? When they left here, where did they go?" It was as though an entirely new path for thought was opening up for the Jamesons. Suddenly, a world they thought impossible had opened and revealed itself to them in a most peculiar way.

"They don't really 'go' anywhere, Dr. Jameson. Rather, they simply exist in their own dimension which compliments ours. It is their awareness of their surroundings that changes. They become aware of the world of spirit and focus their attention in that direction, which is far superior for them since they are without physical bodies. Once they have accepted the transition, their opportunities become limitless. It is a joyful existence on the other side."

I noticed Dr. Jameson reach over to squeeze his wife's hand, a sentimental gesture that touched me very deeply. After all, the Jamesons were not far from traveling that road themselves. But they were novices to the world of spirit. I could not help but feel that in a bizarre way the ghosts had given them hope for their own immortality. Mrs. Jameson smiled as she entered the conversation.

"It seems strange to ask, but what does one do with one's time in that world?"

"Many things you might do here, Mrs. Jameson. You might choose to attend a class, work with children, or plan, with the help of a teacher, the path of your next life. We are all in a learning process, building toward returning home."

"By 'returning home' do you mean Heaven?"

"You could call it Heaven. Language offers poor choices for a description of the eternal but, of course, it is what we have chosen to work with in this reality. The point from which we ventured initially, to learn and grow, is where we will eventually return as advanced, loving beings to the god force which created us and which is a part of each of us. But for most of us, that is many lessons from now."

"Forgive me, Professor; but in my practice, I saw no evidence of life after death. I attended an innumerable count of patients on their deathbeds. I saw nothing that would indicate to me that a spirit was escaping the body at death. As a physician, I must tell you, I have no such awareness of further life without physical bodies. But this experience with ghosts, I admit to complete mystification. I do not consider myself an unintelligent man, Professor. How could I have missed anything this important?"

"Look toward the south wall, Doctor, and tell me what you see."

"The door to the foyer, the buffet, a china cabinet, nothing more."

"Do you see the dining room table?"

"No, of course not, it's behind me!"

"That's my point, Doctor. Focus and perspective, everything falls in the category of perspective. You did not see a world of spirit because you were not looking for it. As your patients lay dying, what were you thinking about?"

"Their comfort, naturally. There was nothing left to be done to save them, so I wanted to make their parting as painless as possible."

"And that was where you directed your attention, Dr. Jameson. That was the way you chose to serve humanity. You have directed your attention toward a very fulfilling life and a need that required your complete dedication. That, of course, was your goal in this lifetime. And, it being a most demanding goal, it is where you have been focused. But something may have gone unnoticed as you attended your dying patients. I have found it to be related by those attending most dying patients because of the confusing circumstance. Were any of them able to communicate with you before their passing?"

"Oh, yes, most were quite coherent. They spoke to me intelligently, seemed more relaxed than usual. And, well, come to think of it, I could never explain . . ."

"Yes, Doctor, please go on."

"Well, often they seemed to be conversing with me and I would respond until they called me by another name, or made reference to something I had no knowledge of. It was as though they were talking to someone I could not see."

"Indeed they were, Doctor. As we cross from this world to the next, we are greeted by those who have gone before us. Or a teacher we have known throughout our eternal learning process will be there to welcome our return. An interesting piece of documented history on this subject is the deaths of Thomas Jefferson and John Adams. Thomas Jefferson died on the Fourth of July, fifty years after the signing of the Declaration of Independence by the Second Continental Congress. Several hours later, in a different state, his good friend and compatriot, John Adams, lay dying. If this alone is not a strain on what you call coincidence, consider this: Adams's last words were "Jefferson lives." Since Adams, in a different state with no advanced form of communication available to him, had no way of knowing of Jefferson's death, it impresses me that Jefferson showed up, looking very much alive, to collect his old friend, so that they could make this journey together."

Dr. Jameson's disapproving glance was classically skeptical. "Certainly there is no proof that Adams saw the spirit of the dead Jefferson. He may have been reacting to some medication, or simple wishful thinking."

"Do you need further proof of the existence of the spirits that traumatized you and turned your household upside down, Doctor?"

"No! Emphatically not! No, no, they were very real. I see your point, Professor. Maybe all there is to see is not visible at all times."

"Eloquently put, Doctor. In a dramatic way, you have been introduced to one of the worlds beyond this dimension. It could be a beginning to a fascinating journey if you should choose to follow the path."

"One of the worlds, Professor? There are more?"

"In this vast universe, it never ceases to amaze me that mankind believes, through the containment of ego alone, that we are the only intelligent beings that exist. How could that logically be? We already know there is so much beyond our short span of reason.

We have knowledge of countless universes, thanks to science, and of billions of stars. But we insist that the only existing intelligence is our own. Do you see the irony in this thought, Doctor? Instead of creative and logical thought leading to creative and logical exploration, we choose to give credence to only what we can sense with meager physical sensation and ability. There is ever so much more!"

I had to laugh as I looked around the table. Mrs. Jameson, Meredith, and Bree sat mesmerized in the play of conversation.

"Meredith, you have never been at a loss for words that I can recall!"

"Your ability to teach fascinates me, Lang."

"It is not superior to your own, my dear."

"Here it comes! The scheduled meeting of the mutual admiration society. They are forever complimenting each other. What they don't know is that they are exactly alike!"

"Bree! Behave yourself."

"It's true, Meredith. It's as though the two of you were molded by the same genius who liked his work so much he decided to do it again. When you compliment each other, you are complimenting yourselves. Now, there's a loophole for egocentric behavior we could all use."

We all had a good laugh over Bree's perspective. I know Meredith and I do reflect each other's attitudes and beliefs. I had attributed it to similar experiences; but, in truth, it went beyond that. We often anticipated each other's actions to the point of responding prior to the event. But expanded awareness was what the world of psychic phenomena was about.

"If I could ask another question." The doctor's tone of voice became quite serious. "I can't help but remember the spirit of the woman weeping in the hallway. She was carrying a child. A Jameson child? There might be descendants of that child, an heir of Philip entitled to this property."

"Your kindness precedes you, Doctor; but there is no heir." Meredith gently explained her statement. "I was curious about the same thing. Tuning in to Amanda, I found she died in child-birth, as many in that time did; and the child, a son, went with her. The house is yours with no other to lay claim to it."

"What a shame." Dr. Jameson responded. The room became quiet with us silently wishing well to a soul from a hundred years ago who rejected its material manifestation. We sat quietly reflecting on Amanda's lost baby.

I broke the silence. "I have been wanting to tell you, I couldn't help but think about my parents when I was working here on Saturday, Doctor. They are both physicians and could never understand my psychic ability or my interest in the paranormal. You helped me to see reality from their point of view, as well. They are well-meaning, giving people, in their own way. It is ironic that someone as close to their world would experience my world. I understood, watching your reactions to all that was happening around you, how differently we perceived reality. Somehow, it made me feel a closeness to my parents that I had never felt before. For that, I wish to thank you, Doctor."

Dr. Jameson seemed rather uncomfortable with sentiment, but I needed to express my feelings.

"Could we pray for the souls that were trapped in this house, Professor, and the child that was never born? Would that help them?" asked Mrs. Jameson.

"Prayer, in whatever form, is always welcome, Mrs. Jameson. The positive energy that flows from us, directed to another soul, can do so much good. Yes, definitely, pray for the spirits, that they find their path. As always, your goodness will be returned to you many times over."

The evening continued with many questions and answers. Bree related how she had seen her parents with our guidance. Mrs. Jameson seemed especially entranced by her description of her parents in another world.

The topic then focused on Meredith. Many in this small town, as well as surrounding communities, already knew of Meredith's ability. She had already given valuable psychic guidance to so many.

Mrs. Jameson was becoming increasingly interested in this phenomena and asked: "How do you know what to say to people?"

"I release my ego, Mrs. Jameson."

She looked puzzled, encouraging Meredith to continue. "The information I give to clients does not come from me. If I feel myself determining answers through my own logic, then I must stop. Usually, after a brief meditation, I can continue. Occasionally, however, it's necessary for me to end a session with a promise to continue at another time. My thought processes must be left out of my readings completely, if they are to be accurate."

"Could you explain exactly how that works?"

"Well, I will try, Dr. Jameson. It's as though I am invited into your awareness. I invest myself into your world, relaying exactly what I see, like a recording machine being played back. An instrument, if you will. I must not add my ideas, or in any way change the picture presented to me. I must remain as the one in the middle, just sending back information. If I can't eliminate my own ego and interpretation from the session, then it's worthless. For that reason, it's very hard for me to read for someone I am close to personally. I am forever trying to divorce my emotions from the situation in order to do an accurate reading. Once I have eliminated ego from the reading, it becomes unbelievably easy. It seems to flow, and then I know I am giving the most that I am capable of."

"Fascinating! I really am learning something new, even in my old age." Dr. Jameson expressed many sentiments throughout the course of the evening. They all seemed to echo the same image, new thoughts, new ideas, a new perspective. As much of my work reaffirmed my reason for this lifetime, I was continually energized by bringing enlightenment to an ever expanding audience of people. It gave me the true sensation of being one with the universe, and one with all life. The reward for finding one's true niche in this world is a sense of belonging in its simplest, most logical state. This is a reward beyond any I could determine for myself. There is a comfort level which, in my experience, develops from the feelings of becoming one with all that is.

A tree, for example, is invested with the same energy found in all life, including myself. I can communicate with it by sending a sense of love and peace that it reciprocates to me in the form of positive energy. Most would find this concept difficult to accept until it is experienced. Then it seems to be the most natural of exchanges. The world need not be one of "them versus us" because in truth, we are all part of each other. We are all part of the energy that exists and flows through all things and all creatures. As a whole, we can only grow; but divided, we are less than we must be.

As such, we must not leave one behind. Those of us having had more evolution in accumulated lifetimes and experiences wait, encourage, and advise those following in our footsteps. For without them, we will go nowhere. Patience and love, forever the greatest teaching aids at our disposal, must be administered liberally to all while they travel their path toward the eternal quest.

And, as we grow, we learn that nothing is terminal. There is no act committed from which we cannot recover. There is no experience from which we will not learn. Some may take more time, or become so ensconced in a difficult occurrence of their lives, that they seem to repeat endlessly and never go beyond that experience. But experience, the finest and most patient teacher, replays itself until the lesson is learned and can finally be put to rest. When we give up on another, we give up on ourselves. It can't be done.

Calvert, my students, my dearest friends are all gifts to me. With the help of the energy of the loving people here, I will complete this journey. My obligation is to return at least a part of the joy I feel here; to lessen the burden of those who can use my knowledge and insights for their own growth. It is my absolute joy to contribute, in any way I can, to the growth of all in our mission of spirituality. And we do that by expanding our knowledge and interpreting what we have learned through our emotions: by understanding our world, our universe. By evolving, starting from whatever point we are at and accepting our lessons; learning what we came to learn, then moving on. In every culture, every religion talks of coming to a point in each life when all seems to be out of one's control. It is the point at which we realize that whatever abated our dilemmas in the past will no longer work. At this point, a major step in individual human evolution, we must let go. We can do nothing else. At this time we realize how much we are a part of everything, of our very environment. Here we stand, unable to come to our own aid, incapable of correcting some terrible problem. We must trust that all will right itself. And so it does. From that point, are we in awe of our god force? Are we amazed and in wonderment of the magnificent power inside of us that has surfaced to come to our aid? We should be. If we recognize this power we summon from deep inside, used to help us in our need, then we will recognize our importance. We will recognize how much we are loved, how much we are able to love and our oneness with all things. This is a great step in evolution. Opening hearts and minds to our true birthright, this is the vocation to which I have devoted my life, a decision I could never regret.

The Jameson experience brought out even more curiosity seekers and an influx of phone calls requesting information, signing up for classes. I convinced Meredith to start a class in psychic awareness at her counseling center. The university did not have the time to liberally address all of the expanded interest in the paranormal brought about by the Jameson haunting. Here was an opportunity to educate, one we could not ignore. Classes were established and filled almost immediately. It was a frantic, but gratifying year.

And all the while, the Angels advanced in their quest to return lost children.

# Chapter 9

A child in Calvert was missing. We had heard on the news that a young girl had disappeared from her home in the middle of the night. A search party formed and for the better part of the day, attempted to find little Carolyn Blaire.

I was teaching a class when I received the news, and cancelled classes for the rest of the day. Carolyn's brother, Jeremy, was one of my students. We all were feeling the family's loss and anxiety. The fact that this was Jeremy's sister made this problem very personal. The Angels were notified and assembled at the counseling center that night. At this point, we had been so used to repeated out-of-body experiences that we could elicit this phenomenon without the aid of sleep. We sat in our "drawing" room, so named for "drawing" spirit from physical confinement. We would, at the same time, take deep cleansing breaths and simply force our spirits up through our bodies and out through the crown chakra. It had become as natural as changing a shirt.

Armed with information on this child, we visualized her; five years old, a redhead, green eyes, with a deeply freckled complexion. She was last seen in her red-and-white polka dot pajamas crawling into bed by her now frantic mother. We found ourselves in her bedroom.

"What are we doing here? I thought this child was lost, not at home!" Meredith seemed surprised to find herself in this place, as we all were.

"Something is wrong. We must have slipped back in time, visualized her so accurately ready for bed that we inadvertently went back in time to her bedtime."

"That's a plausible explanation, Professor, but now what do we do?"

"I'm not sure, Amy. Meredith, what do you see out there?"

Meredith was looking out the bedroom window. "It was a cat."

"Pardon me?"

"It was a cat, Lang. She heard it meowing outside and climbed out on this tree branch, then climbed down the tree to chase after the cat. She wasn't taken, she just left. She followed the cat! I believe she lost her way and can't find her home. That's why we're here. When we think of her, we go to the place she is thinking about. She's thinking about being at home because she's lost and doesn't know how to get back here. Join hands with me. I need combined energy to tune in to her surroundings." We all stood in a circle, meditating and supporting Meredith's effort.

"She's in a woods. Is there a woods around here?"

"Yes, about a half mile from here. Is that where she is?"

"I think so, Mark. She has been there the whole time. She was asleep under a tree, woke up, and is panicking because it's dark. I see her surrounded by trees, sitting on the ground, under a massive oak."

"I know where that large oak tree is."

"Good, let's go."

Instantly, we were standing in a beautifully colored, moonlit autumn woods. Because of her red hair and red polka dot pajamas, Carolyn almost blended with her surroundings. Fortunately, Calvert was experiencing a mild fall, the air was chilled, but not too cold. She sat on the ground sobbing under a monumental oak tree. The cat she followed was in her arms, obviously as scared as Carolyn, picking up on the child's fear and panicking as animals are prone to do. We tried to talk to her, but she did not respond.

"Why can't she hear or see us?"

"She's buried her psychic ability that would allow her to use her sixth sense. Apparently, she has already been taught only to believe what she sees with her eyes, Alex."

"Well, that's great, Professor! How are we going to get her out of here if we can't communicate with her?"

"What? Oh . . . I'm sorry. I was just noticing something. Meredith, move to your left. Just as I thought. The child can't see us, but the cat can!"

"Well, that's a relief! Now, how do we get the cat to talk to her!"

"Please, Alex! Your sarcastic wit has its place somewhere, but not here. Come on kitty, follow Uncle Lang!" I thought if I could get the cat to follow us, Carolyn would, once again, follow the cat. After all, she got her into this mess. The least our feline friend could do was get her out! It was working. Curious as any of her kitty companions, she hopped out of Carolyn's arms and tried to bat at my face.

"Pretty kitty. That's a good kitty; now follow me."

Carolyn had dried her tears, noticing the strange antics of the cat. Curious to find what had inspired this animal's odd behavior, Carolyn got up and started to follow the enchanted kitty.

"That's good. Now all we have to do is lead the cat home."

Were we not a celestial sight! Down the street, around the corner, down six blocks to Carolyn's front yard. A very confused cat followed her instinctive curiosity and seven astral bodies, all beckoning with "Here, kitty, kitty!"

As we approached Carolyn's home, Mrs. Blaire ran from her front door.

"Carolyn!"

"Mama! I got lost!"

"Where have you been?"

"I was lost in the woods. I heard the kitty outside and climbed out my window on the tree to get to her, but she ran. I ran after her, and then I couldn't find my way home."

Mrs. Blaire held her child, half laughing, but trying to chastise her at the same time. "Never, ever leave home like that! Do you understand me? I'm having your father saw off that tree limb! You could have been hurt or lost forever!" She was so happy to see her daughter, the lesson would have to wait.

"The kitty took me home, Mama! She jumped off my lap and led me home! She's so smart! Can we keep her? Please, Mama?"

We not only returned a missing child, but found a home for a stray cat in the attempt. All in a night's work.

Back in the physical world, we laughed over the experience.

"I didn't know you were such an animal enthusiast, Lang!"

"Whatever it takes, Meredith. Whatever it takes!"

News quickly travelled about Carolyn's return and the adoption of a very bright stray cat. As the excitement settled, I got back to work. Reincarnation was next on the agenda for study. The students were ready and eager for this topic. I was apprehensive. I had spoken to Meredith about my fears. We concluded that one of us feeling uneasy could be an overactive imagination, but both of us . . . no, something was about to happen. Bree was looking forward to studying the subject. That was where the problem existed. Somehow, Bree's involvement in the study of reincarnation made both Meredith and me very uncomfortable.

# Chapter 10

"I think she has some sort of past life issue." Meredith began to speculate with the help of her developed sixth sense. "It's that link she has with the Victorian period. You have noticed it, Lang."

"How could I not notice? Her home, her choice of hairstyles, even her clothing is an anachronism in the twentieth century. The only thing she's missing is a bustle!"

"Yes. But you know, many of us display past life links. Somehow, she is too caught up in that century. I am much too close to her to trust my intuition, but I believe something from that time remains unresolved."

"It must be her subconscious intention to resolve it, then."

"Why do you say that, Lang?"

"She's expressed a wish to be regressed to past life when we get to this phase in class. She's reminded me several times, as though something very important needs attention. I don't know, I am anxious to help her, but I sense it may be a difficult experience for her."

"My feelings exactly. However, if this is Bree's path, then it must be followed."

"Tomorrow we start the subject. Would you care to join my 8A.M. class? That's when Bree plans to attend. You might be able to pick up in some detail on what is about to happen. Maybe even head off some disaster?" I said hopefully.

Meredith shook her head and shrugged her shoulders. "I'll do what I can, Lang. You know I will try, but that's the best I can offer at this point."

As she promised, Meredith walked into my classroom just as we were about to begin. She seated herself in the back of the room, next to Bree.

"Reincarnation. The word alone gets quite a reaction from people. Either they are all for it, or vehemently opposed to the concept. In any event, nearly everyone knows what it is; and most have given it thought and have formed some sort of opinion. So, my first attempt at opening this subject for discussion is to throw it out to you. I want to hear from you about what you believe reincarnation is, how the concept makes you feel, and how you think it could potentially affect your lives. We will begin with you, Terry."

"I have read different books on the subject, Professor. They all seem to say the same thing. If reincarnation is real, it's a way for us to experience life from different perspectives in order to become more knowledgeable."

"Good, Terry. Joanne?"

"I have trouble believing in it, Professor. I mean, it seems like a 'Twilight Zone' plot! Why would we want more than one life on earth?"

"O.K., Joanne. Pete, what are your feelings on the subject?"

"I think it could be fun!"

"Could you expand on that, Pete? How do you think reincarnating could be fun?"

"Well, I mean if you get to choose who you will be, where you will be born and what you will look like, I don't know, it just sounds like a lot of fun to me."

"Control over your lifetimes. O.K., I guess that could be fun. Ellen, how do you feel about reincarnating?"

"The truth, Professor, is that it sort of scares me. I don't like thinking about it."

"What about the subject scares you, Ellen?"

"I guess it's too unknown. You know, I'm used to who I am and all the people I'm familiar with."

"So what you are saying is that there are too many out of control variables in the concept of reincarnation."

"That's right. It's too frightening."

"That's what I call fear of the big picture, Ellen. But your fears are valid. Maybe we can dispel some of them for you. Very good. I am happy to know that you have opinions on the subject. Now we will take those and examine them and possibly add others, as well.

Reincarnation is the most accepted belief among humans on this planet. Of all the theories of religious philosophy on the subject of continuing life, it's the most popular. It's also the most logical. If our mission is to become aware and to experience life to its fullest, then it follows that one lifetime would not be adequate for such an endeavor. How, for example, do we live a life in middle class America, and then try to extend our awareness of humanity in other cultures? We have no basis for comparison to empathize with the plight and vexations of people in, say, a third world country from our vantage point. Life takes on a completely different awareness if we are living it versus reading about it. And the lessons of life are more deeply instilled in us when learned through the emotions, rather than from the perspective of a student. For that reason, reincarnation would seem to be a logical choice to gain understanding of the human condition. As beings who reincarnate from one life experience to another, we retain what we have learned in the past. Hopefully, these lessons will serve us in our present life and will accumulate and go on to serve us in future lives. Many books have been written on the subject of reincarnation.

Through the medium of hypnosis, people have encountered past lives and have given validity to the study by pinpointing facts and details of past life which are then verified. People telling of their death experience in a previous lifetime and leading the inquisitor to his or her previous grave, for example. On your way in to class today, you each received a reading list of books that might interest you. They are different books on reincarnation, from the perspective of investigators and people with actual past life recall. Several on the list pertain to practitioners of psychology who use past life therapy in their work. These people have found it beneficial to include emotional examination of past life in attempting to deal with emotional problems in present life. You look rather surprised, Joe."

Once again, Reverend Anderson's son Joe seemed perplexed by the volumes of information on this subject.

"I wasn't aware reincarnation was accepted by people in the field of psychology, Professor."

"It has been accepted by some. Many are still skeptical. But as the pioneers give more and more validity to reincarnation through their work, it will become an accepted method of treatment. Many of you are psychology majors. You know from your study that the subconscious mind is a reservoir of stored information. That being the case, it is necessary to root out stored information that affects behaviors. Past life information is no different in that it colors the way we interpret and react to various stimuli in our lives. No study of reincarnation would be complete without a proper understanding of hypnosis. Without the aid of hypnosis, we would be unable, in most instances, to reliably tap into a past life. For that reason, we will preface our study of reincarnation with an understanding of hypnosis. How it works, what it can do, etc. Margaret, do you have a question?"

"Yes, Professor. Will we be hypnotizing someone so that we can see a past life first hand?"

I saw Bree's face light up with this question. There was no doubt in my mind that she would volunteer to be put under. "You are jumping ahead of me, Margaret; but, yes, I see no reason why we should not explore this subject to that extent.

To continue, hypnosis is a method used to manipulate the subconscious mind. The part of the brain that we refer to as the subconscious spans all but a small portion of the brain. The consciousness, on the other hand, is a small portion, about the size of a half dollar. Everything you have ever experienced, either actively or verbally, is stored in your subconscious.

When someone says something to you or you find yourself in a particular situation, your response depends on the data you have stored on that subject. You are asked your opinion of medical testing on animals, for example. Your brain scans the data banks of your subconscious, and your response is linked to your history with animals. Did you grow up on a farm where slaughtering animals for food was a common occurrence? Or rather, was one of your parents a veterinarian who taught you to love and respect animals for their individual beauty and intelligence? These lifestyles and opinions, as you grew up, would certainly color your response to the question of lab testing on animals.

That's only one example. Everything we encounter or learn is dealt with in this manner. What information have I stored? How does what I know apply to my current concern? Subconscious data is the reason why no two people, witnessing the same scene, will describe it exactly the same way. We photograph with our eyes, then take the print to our subconscious, run it through that database for a reaction, response, or otherwise appropriate conclusion.

The subconscious mind cannot reason; that's not its job. It merely stores and offers data as we consciously request it. The fact that the subconscious cannot reason offers the hypnosis practitioner endless opportunity.

But I digress. Let's start with a basic understanding of hypnosis and go on from there. Allison, you have been hypnotized to make dentistry a more palatable, excuse the pun, experience?" My puns, even though I insist they are strictly accidental, cause groaning responses throughout my classes.

"Yes, Professor. Without Meredith's help, I would be a basket case. She hypnotized me once a week while my dental appointments continued. With her help, I didn't even need anesthesia."

"Tell us about the experience from your perspective, Allison."

"Well, I would go over to the counseling center Monday evenings. Meredith had me sit in a big overstuffed chair. The first time she put me under, she did some sort of exercise having me open and close my eyes as she counted. Then, when I became very tired from this, she started to talk to me, kind of painting a peaceful relaxing picture. I don't remember much after that. When my sessions were over, I just went home.

Meredith had asked for the name and phone number of my dentist. She apparently explained who she was and what she had done and gave Dr. Giles a code word that he could use to reactivate my hypnotic trance. Then, when he was finished, he would wake me up with another code word. Meredith had told him to always tell me that I would feel fine and alert as he was bringing me out of my trance. It seemed miraculous. I had always had a fear of the dentist, and I needed a lot of dental care. I would get so panicky that anesthetics would have no effect on me. Prior to my meeting Meredith, I suffered tremendously with my dental problems. But after she started to use hypnosis to help me, I not only felt nothing, I remembered nothing. And, according to Dr. Giles, I seemed to heal faster, too."

"Thank you, Allison. Meredith, would you care to fill in the details of Allison's story and explain the process?"

"Certainly, Professor." In the classroom, Meredith always addressed me respectfully. And I always stifled the urge to laugh! She made her way to my podium and once again I had the privilege of taking a break and watching a master at work.

"Hypnosis certainly can seem miraculous. Hypnosis is a method of working with the largest part of the human brain, the subconscious. In order to access the subconscious, we must put the conscious mind to sleep. After that is accomplished, we then have a direct link to the subconscious where we can begin innumerable tasks. Since the subconscious mind cannot reason, it generally accepts any data offered to it as fact. Allison's need to lose her fear of the dentist, as well as not feel pain, was addressed in two stages. Once Allison was hypnotized, I reprogrammed her acceptance of her dentist as someone who wished to help her rather than someone who caused her pain. That done, I gave Allison a post-hypnotic suggestion that, with a trigger word, she would re-enter her trance state and feel nothing as the dentist worked on her teeth. I also informed Allison that another trigger word would be used by her dentist to awaken her when he was finished. I use somnambulistic hypnosis. There are subtle forms of hypnosis that do not require as deep a trance. However, since my work leans more toward the discovery of life's mysteries, I find somnambulistic hypnosis more suitable."

"What does that phrase mean, Meredith?"

"Literally, Amy, it means the walking sleep. A person who walks in his or her sleep is in a deep trance. Once I feel a subject is sufficiently in trance, I test the subject by establishing a comfort level in a normally uncomfortable position. For example, I may tell the subject to raise one arm at a ninety-degree angle to the body. This is usually an uncomfortable position, but with some suggestions, and in deep trance, the subject can be quite comfortable in this position for any length of time. I may tell the subject, for example, that this is no longer an arm, but a piece of wood. With this suggestion, the arm becomes rigid, resembling an unbending piece of wood. I suggest that the wood is resting in a good place, and the subject leaves the arm in this position as I continue to talk to him, and divert his attention to other things. Noting how the subject is reacting to his arm at a ninety-degree angle with the passage of time tells me how deep his trance really is. If it looks as though the arm is faltering or that the subject is beginning to display signs of discomfort, then we need to deepen the trance.

Or I might suggest that the subject close his eyes, then tell him that when I count from one to ten, he will find he is unable to open them again.

If the subject passes simple tests, such as these, I then might try to regress him to his childhood in this lifetime. Depending on the depth of the trance, I should be able to offer any date in the subject's childhood, count him back to that time, and have him relate his experience to me. You have a question, Margaret?"

"Yes, Meredith. Does the subject remember every detail of the day he is regressed to?"

"Good question, Margaret. To have the subject recall as much detail as possible is the goal of this exercise. Again, the deeper the trance, the more will be remembered. Or more accurately, experienced, since in trance the subject feels he actually is reliving events. Extensive recollection is a product of the depth of the subject's trance. Recalling childhood activity in great detail tells me that my subject is ready for further work.

That question brings a situation to mind you might find amusing. I worked with a gentleman who wished to be regressed to past life. This young man had extensive psychic ability. He was able to recall past life while semiconscious or in a relaxed alpha state, but the recollection came in the form of images only. He would seat himself in front of a mirror and watch scenes of his lifetimes play out before him. But there was no dialogue, and all he was left with were impressions.

As I do with each new client, I had him fill out a questionnaire before beginning our first session. One of the questions on that form has to do with recalling upsetting events in one's life. If, for example, you were involved in an accident, I would not want to bring you back to that time to re-experience the accident. If you can tell me approximately when it occurred, I will navigate you around that time during your present life regression.

After he completed this form, we began our session. Ted turned out to be a highly responsive subject. Hypnotizing him was quite easy. In that first session, we worked our way to regression in this lifetime. Armed with the paper telling me about any pitfalls in Ted's past, I regressed him to age five. At this point, since Ted is the first-born American in his family, he spoke to me in a combination of English and Italian. I asked him to describe the day. He told me he was going downstairs to play with his new toys. They were in the playroom just past the kitchen. He walked down the stairs and discovered a fire smoldering in the kitchen. Naturally, for a five-year-old boy, this is a frightening discovery. Ted began to scream and cry uncontrollably. Over his screams, I loudly objected to his surroundings and removed him from this place. It took a total of half an hour to regain control over Ted's emotions and redirect him to a place of safe memories.

After our session ended that day, I asked Ted why he had neglected to tell me about the fire he discovered when he was five years old. Ted gazed back at me with an amazed look on his face.

"Fire? I never discovered any fire!" he flatly stated while looking at me innocently.

"I beg to differ with you, Ted; but I just spent a good thirty minutes calming you down after discovering that fire at age five!"

Ted was completely baffled. He had no conscious recollection of such an event. Later that afternoon, I received a phone call from Ted. He was at his mother's house. She had explained to him that when they first came to the United States, they moved in with his mother's sister. He did remember living with his Aunt Jo. She also explained that Ted had indeed discovered a fire starting in the kitchen of his aunt's house when he was five years old.

He screamed and ran back to his mother on the second floor.

I explained to Ted that sometimes we bury frightening memories. So you see, even though the conscious mind may forget important details of our lives, the subconscious never forgets. Nick, you have a question?"

"Is hypnosis dangerous in any way, Meredith?"

"Hypnosis is a formidable tool, Nick. Things that can be accomplished with its use have only the boundaries of imagination. I would have to say yes, it can be very dangerous."

"Do you mean someone could go under and never wake up again?"

"No, Nick, it's not dangerous in that way. Hypnosis is an enhanced form of sleep. When a hypnotist puts you in a deep trance, you give him permission to communicate with your subconscious and you are instructed to respond to his voice only to keep you focused. If the hypnotist were to stop communicating with you, you would simply fall into a normal sleep and wake up in your own time. The way in which hypnosis can be dangerous is through trickery."

"I don't understand."

"I'll explain, Nick. Better yet, allow me to demonstrate. Professor?"

And I was so relaxed just sitting there listening! Oh well, back to work. I made my way back to the front of the class and seated myself in a chair in front of Meredith.

"Your professor has much experience with hypnosis. As a person becomes familiar with hypnosis and comfortable with the process, it takes less and less time to induce a trance. Therefore, Professor Evans, please close your eyes, take a deep breath and imagine yourself peacefully floating on a raft. It's a beautiful summer day, a lovely blue lake, complete with sunshine and cotton ball clouds. And we will count back from ten to one, each number relaxing you into a deeper and deeper sleep. Ten, all you want to do is sleep; nine, deeper and deeper asleep; eight, . . . seven, . . . six, . . . five, . . . four, . . . three, . . . two, . . . one-and asleep. You may open your eyes, Professor. How do you feel?"

"Relaxed."

"Good. Take a deep breath. I'm going to hand you a hunting knife. We're in the forest. You never know what might come upon you in the forest." Meredith turned toward the class to show them there was nothing in her hand. As she handed the imaginary knife to me: "Professor, there is a poisonous snake at your feet. It's about to strike. Kill it." With that, I thrust my imaginary knife down in the direction of the attacking snake.

"Very good, Professor. How are you feeling today?"

"Quite well, thank you."

"You're still holding that knife, aren't you?"

"Yes."

"There's a puppy at your feet. Kill it."

"No."

"Professor, I said there is a puppy at your feet. Kill it."

"I will not."

"And why not, Professor?"

"It's only a puppy. It won't harm you."

"Very good, Professor. I will snap my fingers and you will sleep. No sound will disturb you until I snap my fingers a second time. At that time, you will, once again, respond to my voice only. Is that clear?"

"Yes."

"Good." With that Meredith snapped her fingers and I fell into a much appreciated nap.

"Your Professor loves puppies!" Everyone began to laugh, then cautiously quieted looking over at their sleeping professor.

"Don't worry. He can't hear any of us. He's responding to the suggestion that he sleep undisturbed until he hears me snap my fingers again. What we have demonstrated is that one cannot force someone to do anything he would not ordinarily do, not even under hypnosis. However, a person can be tricked. If I were to tell him, for example, that the puppy was a dangerous snake . . . The subconscious mind, subjected to the will of the hypnotist, believes everything it is told without question. Why? Because it cannot reason. Could someone use trickery to get you to do something under hypnosis that you would not ordinarily do? Absolutely. For that reason, I caution you only to allow yourselves to be hypnotized by someone you know to be reputable; and if there is any question, to bring a friend with you who will remain awake and aware of the proceedings."

"Since we have your professor in trance, why don't we have some fun? Professor?" Meredith snapped her fingers and I opened my eyes.

"Professor, I would like you to close your eyes for me. We are about to take a journey in time. I would like to regress you into your childhood. Do I have your permission?"

"Yes."

"Good. Take a deep breath and our journey begins. At this time, you're forty-five years old, is that correct?"

"Yes."

"I will count to five. When I reach the number five, you will be eighteen years old. Do you understand?"

"Yes."

"One, you are moving backward through time. Two, ten years have passed. Three, now twenty. Four, now twenty-five years have passed. Five, plus two more. How old are you?"

"I am eighteen."

"Describe where you are and what you are doing."

"It's the day of my high school graduation. I still haven't decided on a university. My father is anxious for me to go to his. I don't want to be a doctor. I . . ."

"Very good, just rest and take a deep breath. Good. Now we will go back further. This time when I count to five, you will be ten years old and it's Christmas day. One, you are again moving backward through time. Two, three years have passed. Three, and another two years. Four, two more years have passed. Five, and you are what age?"

"Ten."

"What are you doing and what do you see?"

"It's Christmas morning. No one's up yet, but I can't sleep. I just know Mom bought me that bicycle I've been wanting; but I can't find it anywhere! Shhhhh! They're awake and on their way down. They can't find me here! They'll know I was looking for that bike!"

"Pay attention to me, please. I want to see how well you sign your name. I'm giving you a piece of paper and a pen. Sign your name for me, please."

Meredith, using an available overhead projector, displayed my signature at age ten. A low chatter developed as the students noted the changes in a signature not as yet matured. They had seen my signature previously signed on many notes done on their research. This was certainly different from what they were used to seeing.

"Thank you. Please close your eyes, take a deep breath. We will go back in time again. This time when I reach the number five, you will be six years old. One, you are traveling back in time. Two, one year has passed. Three, now two years have passed. Four, you are almost there now. And, five; how old are you?"

"I am six."

"Where are you and what are you doing?"

"I start first grade today! I'm a big boy now!"

"Can you write your name?"

"Sure!"

"Would you do that for me?"

"Uh huh."

What the class saw on the overhead projector was a child's scrawl, doing his best to print his name.

"Thank you. Once more, I will have you take a deep breath. This time you will go back to age four. When we reach the number five you will be four years old. One, back in time. Two, relaxed and moving back through time. Three, you are almost there, only two more years to go. Four, just about there, you're doing very well. And five; how old are you?"

A grown man with the mannerisms of a child, raised four fingers in response. Students watched in amazement.

"Can you talk to me?"

"Uh huh."

"Could you write your name on a piece of paper?"

"No."

"Why not?"

"I don't know how. I can draw.

"What is your favorite thing to do?"

"Play catch with Daddy."

"Very good. I want you to rest and relax. Close your eyes. I will count, this time to ten. When I reach the number ten, you will be forty-five years old, sitting in your classroom at Fields University. One, coming back slowly. Everything's fine. Two, take deep breaths. You will feel fine. Three. Four. Easy does it. Five. Six. Feeling good. Seven. Eight. You are almost there now. Nine. Ten. How old are you?"

"Forty-five."

"Good. I want you to listen to me very carefully. My objective here is to show your students the power of the human subconscious. Do I have your permission to conduct this experiment?"

"Yes."

"I'm going to touch your arm with a hot poker. You will feel no pain, but the poker will cause a blister to raise on your arm. Is that clear?"

"Yes."

With my permission, Meredith took an ordinary pencil and touched my arm. Done without mirrors, a blister formed just as she said it would. Meredith gave them time as the students filed passed to see for themselves. The classroom reverberated with astonishment. They had watched me blister with only a suggestion and the touch of a pencil that I believed to be a hot poker.

"That's fine. I will now apply some ice and the blister will disappear, leaving the skin unscarred."

With that, Meredith applied a balled-up tissue, and as she predicted, the blister disappeared leaving no scar. Again, students filed past to view what seemed to be the impossible. And yet, it happened before their eyes.

"I am going to give you a post-hypnotic suggestion. After I

have taken you out of your trance, I will say the word fascinating. The word fascinating will have a one time and immediate effect on you. After hearing the word fascinating, you will succumb to an incredible urge to remove both of your shoes and both of your socks. You will then place your socks inside your shoes and put them on top of the desk in front of you. Is that clear?"

"Yes."

"Also, once you are awake, you will remember nothing of this session. Do you understand?"

"Yes."

"Good. I'm going to bring you out of trance now. We will do this by counting to five. When I reach the number five you will be wide awake, rested, and feeling fine. One, come up slowly, please. Two, feeling good. Three, you're coming awake now. Four, almost there. And five, awake!"

"Great. Did I make an awful fool of myself?"

"No, but you were an adorable baby!"

My students, amused with the show, applauded and laughed.

"Well, that's just great!"

"You may return to your seat now, Professor. As usual, you make a <u>fascinating</u> subject."

I reached my desk, sat down, bent over in my chair, not noticing every student's eyes on me, and started to untie my shoes. I took them off, giving no thought to what I was doing, removed my socks, tucked my socks neatly inside my shoes, and put them on the desk in front of me. Looking up, I then noticed the entire classroom staring at me! I'd been had! I put both hands over my eyes and uttered a groan of embarrassment! The students roared with laughter.

"All right. Have your fun."

"What we have demonstrated here is the absolute power

and control the subconscious mind has over the conscious. The professor would not ordinarily remove his shoes in class, and yet because the thought was firmly planted in his subconscious he was unable to resist. Just as you would sneeze without thinking about why, a post-hypnotic suggestion placed in the subconscious during deep trance must be carried out with no thought given to it. Professor, would you care to take your class again?"

"Thank you, Meredith. I have no recollection of the trance. It seemed as though five minutes had passed instead of thirty as I see by my watch. Let's open this discussion and answer your questions."

"That blister, Professor Evans. Did you feel any pain?"

"Blister? Oh, no, in fact I was not aware that had been done until you mentioned it. That is a dramatic demonstration, isn't it?"

"But how?"

"We have studied in class the absolute power and creative ability of the human mind. A suggestion given to the subconscious is accepted as fact, because the subconscious is incapable of reason. That done, it causes the effect. So you see from this demonstration that we are all in control of our environment, our bodies, our health. In fact, there is nothing in our world we do not control.

"So you are saying that the power of your mind caused a blister to form on your arm?"

"Yes, Mark. And that very same power caused a healing. It all makes sense when you consider that no medicine works the same way on two individuals. A method of healing may be effective on one person, but not another. The belief in a doctor or the prescription he offers is more important in the healing of a human being than the medication itself."

"Then why do we all succumb to some illness? Why don't we just obliterate cancer and heart disease?"

"Why, indeed, Margaret! You tell me why we don't. What do you think?"

"I don't know! Why would people want to suffer needlessly?"

"Good! You used the word needlessly. Is it really needless suffering, or does the person have a goal in mind, an objective? Or is this person creating without the knowledge of their own power? I would say all possibilities exist. Surely, we create in order to learn. After all, in this plane we call the earth phase of development, our greatest teacher is our own ability to feel. We create an empathy in ourselves when we experience something rather than when we simply see it happen to another."

"But why would anyone want to be sick on purpose?"

"You're viewing things from a singular physical perspective. When we put time and space and our own existence in proper proportion to eternity, it is as a flame, ignited, snuffed, and ignited again. We can do nothing to permanently destroy energy. We use and reuse it many times over in the pursuit of true knowledge."

"So we use illness as a teacher, Professor?"

"Carol, we use everything as a teacher. But, again, we digress. The subject today is reincarnation. We have demonstrated the effectiveness of hypnosis as a tool in accessing one's past lives. Tomorrow we will regress our first subject. As I have notified all of my classes, we will be conducting this in the school's auditorium to accommodate everyone, and a closed circuit television will be used to magnify and amplify the demonstration."

Bree, Meredith, and I had a late supper together that night.

# Chapter 11

“Are you certain you're ready to experience your incarnations, Bree?

“Oh, yes, Meredith! I have always wanted to find past lives.”

“One in particular you keep reliving, isn't that right?” The seriousness of my tone made Bree slightly uneasy.

“Well, I guess . . . the Victorian period.” Bree had told us previously of an experience linking her with the Victorian Era. The fact that the home she lived in was designed in that century could have given her the type of comfort level she experienced with this period in history. But a strange occurrence at the age of ten was anything but comfortable in the beginning, and all too strange for such a young child.

As Bree had put it, she had been on an outing with her classmates. Their class field trip took them to the Museum of Science and Industry in Chicago, Illinois. The museum itself is designed to entice children. There they are encouraged to explore, hands on. Affectionately known as the "push button" museum, many things can be operated with the help of inquisitive little hands. Bree had wandered off on her own and in a corner of the museum, she found a life-size exhibit of a darkened street at the turn of the century. The street was fabulously realistic with cobblestones and gas lamps, lined with shops and a theater. Female mannequins properly bustled, corseted, and draped in Victorian finery, were strategically placed in dress shop windows to add to the effect of the period. At first glance, the young Bree was unable to catch her breath. The sensation of recognition was so strong as to unexpectedly knock the wind out of her. After a few minutes recovery time, a sense of joy and peace swept over her, as well as a longing to return to this time period, a nostalgic longing to return home. A feeling resurfaced which she has never been without since that experience.

"I believe you have some unfinished business during the Victorian period. Do you really want to get into this before a group of students? I mean, maybe we should be exploring this lifetime with a bit more privacy."

"I trust you, Meredith. After all, how bad can it be? I have always had these nostalgic feelings that I left something behind."

"Or someone," Meredith said gently.

"Yes, or someone." Bree's wistful tone added inspiration for us to do our best. We would open these insistent memories and seal them properly this time. At least we would try.

Hours fleeted into the next day, and before I was even aware so much time had passed, I was summoned to the auditorium for our demonstration. Bree was already seated on the stage. Meredith stood beside her. The closed circuit television equipment had been placed strategically. All they were waiting for was me. I entered from the back of the auditorium. As I climbed the stairs to the stage, I was met with thunderous applause. I went to test the microphone: "We haven't done anything yet!"

A low rumble of laughter made me feel right at home. My, but there were far more than just my students in this auditorium! Every seat was filled with very little standing room left. I looked over at Meredith and Bree. Meredith was her usual confident self. Bree, however, looked as though she would have preferred to be anywhere else. "Are you all right with this, Bree? I can fill in for you if you have changed your mind."

"No, I'm fine. I just didn't expect to see so many people."

I turned to the mike. "Bree was just mentioning that she hadn't expected to see so many in this audience. I am always uplifted by the numbers of people interested in this subject, even if they do not admit to it openly. Still, knowledge is what we are here to gain and so, Ladies and Gentlemen, if we may have your attention and complete quiet, please."

They were ready and interested. You could have heard a pin drop.

"Meredith, I think we are ready."

Meredith turned to face Bree, gave her a wink and squeezed her hand. "Bree, I want you to take a nice deep breath. Good. Now, close your eyes and let the breath out slowly, counting backward from ten. Excellent. Relax completely. Feel as though you are sinking into that chair. And we will begin."

It took approximately fifteen minutes to put Bree into a trance at a sufficient depth. Meredith, manipulating Bree's subconscious, moved Bree through her adolescence and childhood in this lifetime. With the help of the overhead projector and closed circuit television, the audience was able to view Bree's changing handwriting, as well as changing facial expressions. They seemed mesmerized by what they were witnessing.

"You're doing fine, Bree. Now I want you to breathe deeply

and relax. This time, I will count from one to ten. When I reach the number ten, you will find that you are in a different lifetime. You will at no time be in any danger or experience any discomfort. You will see things clearly, as an observer and you will be able to relate to me what you are seeing. Also, your memories of that lifetime will be unleashed and you will be able to answer any questions pertaining to the life you find yourself in. Is that clear?"

"Yes."

"Fine." With that, Meredith started to count very slowly, encouraging Bree to descend into another life. Before too long the expression on Bree's lovely face seemed to come alive with recognition. And, before our eyes, her face began to change ever so subtly. This was no longer Bree.

"Tell me what you see, please."

"Oh, I'm at home! I'm home, finally!" Tears started to well in her eyes.

"Stay apart from this experience, please. I want you to view it as a spectator. I do not want you to relive it." These directions were apparently difficult for Bree to stay with. Although she tried to comply, Bree's emotions got the best of her and she described what must have been a magical life in the year 1895.

"My name is Beth, . . . Beth Sterling. I live with my aunt and uncle in Downer Woods, Illinois. They took me in when I was ten, after my parents died of yellow fever. Uncle John was my father's brother. Uncle John says I remind him of my father more every day! They raised me as though I were theirs. They are so good to me. I have never wanted for anything. We are in the parlor. This is my favorite room. We only use it when we have guests. The chairs are curved wood, carved and gilded. There are windows on three walls with beautiful lace curtains that the sun dances through. Everything is done in pastels, pinks and soft greens. It's so lovely and light in here, you can't help but be happy! I am eighteen. I hope to be engaged soon! His name is Christopher Tait. He will be here any minute! We have kept company for a year now. He must ask my uncle for his blessing on our marriage. I don't know what Uncle John will say. He is so strict and he wants me to go to college. Really, what does a girl need with college! But Christopher has a wonderful future in his family's business. He has studied for years to become an architect and the structures he designs are beautiful ornate buildings. He is so talented! I will be well taken care of."

"Take a deep breath. I will count from one to five and I want you to move ahead an hour or two beyond Christopher's arrival and meeting with your uncle." Meredith counted slowly and deliberately. "Did Christopher see your uncle?"

"Yes. They are coming out of the library right now. Oh my! Oh goodness!"

"What is happening, Beth?"

"He gave his blessing! I am engaged!"

"As I count to ten, you will move ahead, Beth, to your wedding day." Meredith counted slowly and methodically giving Beth time to adjust. "One, two, three, four, five, six, seven, eight, nine, ten. Tell me about this day, Beth."

At this time, Bree, reliving the life of Beth Sterling, was visibly shaken. She was clearly experiencing something troubling, feelings obviously not related to the joy of a young woman on her wedding day. Meredith looked over at me and shook her head. I felt as though I should have stopped Bree from reliving this experience, but she had been so insistent. At this point, I could do nothing but hope for the best.

"We had planned this day for eight months. Everything is ready. But . . . I feel so strange. I feel like I am about to experience something horrible, rather than my beautiful wedding. Aunt Mae has spent so much time with decorations and flowers, how could anything possibly go wrong? And yet, I feel as though I'm about to take a walk toward a guillotine, rather than down the aisle to be united with my Christopher. Aunt Mae is calling me downstairs. A messenger has been sent from the Tait home."

"Take a deep breath. Rest and relax. I want you to move ahead to the time after you have spoken to the messenger." Meredith was trying to move this along so as not to prolong the agony. "What has happened, Beth?"

"It's Chris . . . Oh, no, Christopher!" With that, Bree broke down in tears.

"Listen to me. I want you to take a deep breath and remove yourself from these feelings. I want you to envision this scene as though it were a play acted on a stage. Simply tell me what you see."

Composing herself bravely, Bree, or more accurately, Beth, told a tragic heart-wrenching tale of illness and death.

"It's our wedding day." Beth began stoically. "Christopher's mother sent a messenger to the house. I am to go to him at once. He has taken ill. He hasn't been right since he started that treatment! I told him I didn't like the changes in him and that I thought the treatment should stop. But he can be so stubborn! And he couldn't seem to stop."

"What kind of treatment, Beth?"

"Alphonse Tait, Christopher's father, suffered horribly from consumption. It took years of terrible suffering before he died a crippled wasted man. That disease frightens Christopher so! Christopher found a physician who told him that a medicine would benefit him and keep him from contracting consumption as his father had. He has been taking it for months now. The Doctor told him to take Aiken's tonic pills twice a day. Then he was to smoke the substance in a pipe at least once a day. He started to look so flushed as though he were suffering from a fever and he gained a lot of weight. I told him he should stop, and he tried, but . . ."

"But, what?"

"It was as though he could not stop. I am so afraid to go over there. I just know something awful is going to happen."

"What is in these pills and the tobacco, Beth?"

"People use it all the time. You can purchase it freely at the apothecary. The doctor says it will do no harm, but I have felt that was not true. It is something called arsenic."

"Arsenic?" A low rumble was heard moving through the audience as they realized Christopher had been poisoning himself.

"Yes."

"All right. I want you to take a deep breath and move forward to the time after you have seen Christopher. What is happening now?"

"No! No, no, no! He's gone! I was too late!" Bree, or Beth's tears were uncontrollable. She wept hysterically while Meredith sternly gave orders for her to leave this lifetime, trying desperately to be heard by this emotionally distraught young woman. The whole scene was heartbreaking. Finally, Meredith got through and rapidly invoked healing words as she brought Bree back through the years to the present.

"I will count to ten. As I reach the number ten you will awaken with no memory of what has transpired here. Is that clear?"

"Yes."

"Take a deep breath. You are feeling fine. You will awaken refreshed and in good spirits."

With that Meredith began the count. ". . . five, six, seven, eight, nine, ten-and awake!"

Bree looked bewildered as she awoke to feel the tears that stained her cheeks. She looked at me questioningly. The audience sat silently; no one moved. I explained to the audience that we had recorded the conversation they had just witnessed, and that I would attempt to verify the facts and report our findings to them in another assembly. Everyone seemed exhausted after this ordeal. I checked my watch to find that we had been engaged for a little over an hour. I thanked everyone for their attendance and dismissed the audience. They all seemed shaken as they silently filed out of the auditorium. I went offstage and shut down the microphones. Returning to Bree and Meredith, I joined them in conversation.

"What exactly happened?" Bree questioned us looking confused.

"You remember none of this, Bree?"

"She was in such a deep trance, Lang. I am certain she will remember none of it." Meredith stated, relieved by her own words.

"Bree, you had a very tragic experience in your life in the nineteenth century. It was very sad. We will fill you in, but it is best that you do not have conscious recollection."

"I thought something might be wrong when I felt the tears on my cheeks." Noticing our obvious looks of concern, Bree continued. "I'm all right, really. The two of you look as though you have just been at someone's deathbed!"

Meredith and I looked at each other. "Are you sure you remember nothing?"

"Yes, I'm sure, Lang."

"Good. Let's go get a cup of coffee." I was rewinding the tape in the tape recorder. "We have a lot of work to do, and it's best we talk and make some plans."

A small coffee shop in Calvert specialized in a variety of exotic coffees. I would have been more comfortable with its decor if it had not been so Victorian. Nevertheless, we ordered coffee and began a long discussion. Meredith and I told Bree of the ordeal she had just been through and of the tragic life story of Beth Sterling. Oddly, she seemed unaffected and not at all surprised.

"It's rather interesting to me, Bree, that none of this seems to be coming as a surprise to you."

"I have more of a conscious sense of that lifetime than you realize. If you were to put me back under, you would discover that Beth also passed away at a rather young age. Beth died of the last epidemic of yellow fever in 1905. She had made a fateful trip to St. Louis. It was her last trip."

"Bree, how long have you had this recollection?"

"It just came to me, Meredith. But I know it's accurate. It feels as though I were telling you something that happened last week, rather than over ninety years ago. It's all very clear in my memory."

"We have apparently unleashed memories into your consciousness. I hope you are all right with the reality of these recollections. You would tell us if you felt disturbed by them, wouldn't you?"

"Yes, of course, Meredith. I feel as though I needed to recall that lifetime. I just don't know why."

"Well, I'm canceling classes for tomorrow. We are going to Downer Woods, Illinois. We have to verify these facts. I should have a map of Illinois in my briefcase." I fumbled through some research papers looking for a map. "Here it is. Downer Woods is about a three-hour drive from here. I will drive. Let's leave at about seven tomorrow morning."

That evening, Meredith and I had supper alone. Bree was left at her home with a promise to retire early. She looked emotionally and physically drained.

"It's clear to me, Lang. Bree has never gotten over the trauma of that lifetime. It's always been a mystery to me why someone as lovely and sweet as she is would be spending her life alone. I have never known her even to accept one date."

"Maybe she expects to find Christopher again."

"That's what I was thinking."

The drive to Downer Woods was not one of our usual jovial outings. In fact, we were all so serious and pensive, the trip was becoming long and uncomfortable.

Part of the time we spent listening to the tape from the session the day before. I had already taken notes from it, but I felt Bree should hear the tape, and she agreed. Finally, we reached Downer Woods and looked through a phone book hoping to find a museum or historical society to help us tap into Downer Woods' colorful past. The Downer Woods Historical Society was only a few short blocks from where we stopped.

The building that housed the museum was an impressive, turreted, converted Victorian home. The resident curator, Mrs. Ellen Grenling, greeted us enthusiastically.

"Oh, the nineteenth century, that is my personal favorite. We had some wonderful families in Downer Woods at that time. There's an archive of photos, letters, and various documentation, as well as copies of the local newspaper. Also, we keep the abstracts of each house from that period in the same library."

"Abstracts?"

"Yes, Meredith, those are recordings of homes, who built them, and who lived in them. Abstracts were used before the development of title companies." Bree's knowledge of nineteenth century America and its customs was impressive. She shared information through an obviously loving and crystal-clear recollection.

"Most of the Victorian homes were built by a Chicago architectural firm, as was this one now occupied by the historical society. The family who started that firm were residents of Downer

Woods. It was the architectural firm of Tait and Sons." Mrs. Grenling cheerfully informed us of Downer Woods' most prominent family. "Their Gothic and ornate Victorian buildings were the envy of many firms and they became widely known throughout the Midwest."

At that point nothing surprised us. But we needed to see some records for ourselves. "Could we have access to the library, Mrs. Grenling?"

"Of course, Professor Lang. If you walk through those doors, you will find a staircase on your right. The library is on the second floor. If you should find any photographs or articles you need copies of, we would be happy to reproduce them for you. And if you have any questions, please feel free to call me at my extension. It's listed on the phone you will find on the desk in the library."

Filing cabinets were labeled by year. We found several from the late nineteenth century. Each of us chose a cabinet and began our search.

"Look at this." Meredith spoke first, holding a very old newspaper. She began to read. "The Downer Gazette, 1887. It says: 'Downer Woods welcomes its newest resident, Miss Elizabeth Alice Sterling. Miss Sterling will be living with her aunt and uncle, John and Mae Sterling, who are to raise her since the child has been recently orphaned. We send regards to Beth, as she is known to those who love her, and her new family. We wish them a joyous union and future together in Downer Woods.'"

"Well, it seemed to be a charming town. You look a little pale, Bree."

"I . . . it's all so real!"

"Should we continue this another day?"

"No, Meredith. I'm all right. Please. Let's go on."

Another article told of the Tait family and their thriving

architectural firm. An advertisement in the Gazette flatly stated that no one should consider another company to entrust the building of their most precious acquisition, an exquisitely styled home. This article mentioned the newest Tait to finish study in architectural design and join the firm at age twenty-four. His name was Christopher Allen Tait.

I began looking through a drawer filled with abstracts and found the Sterling home. It seemed that Beth's Aunt Mae and Uncle John lived in the house since their wedding which was also celebrated at that residence. The abstract also documented the date in 1887 when Beth came to live with them.

"So weddings in the Sterling house must have been a family tradition."

"I've found the wedding announcement and a picture. Oh, Bree! You must look at this photograph! Beth had long dark hair, but it's your face!" Meredith was clearly amazed with the resemblance.

Bree walked over and looked over Meredith's shoulder. "He was handsome, wasn't he."

"Yes, Dear. You made a beautiful couple."

"Oh, no. Here it is!"

"What, Lang?"

"I've found a file of obituaries. Christopher was twenty-five years old. There is an article here with the obituary. It says he died of unknown causes on his wedding day."

"Unknown causes! He was poisoned, for heaven's sake!"

"Well, Meredith, they obviously weren't aware their so-called medication was really poison. The article mentions his distraught fiancé, Elizabeth Sterling; and asks for prayers for her recovery from such a terrible loss." I continued through the files of obituaries and found an article from the year 1905. "Look, I've found Beth's obituary."

"Beth's obituary?"

"You're recollections are right, Bree. Ten years later, almost to the day, Beth died of yellow fever after returning from a trip to New Orleans. The article says that Beth had been anxious to see her cousins. She had not seen them since her parents had died and her aunt and uncle planned a trip as a surprise. She returned with a very high fever and other symptoms. The fever seemed to subside a few days later, then raged again. The young woman became jaundiced and died within a week of returning home.

The article goes on to say how Beth had been despondent since the death of her fiancé, Christopher Tait, ten years prior. The once energetic delightful young woman had become morose and introspective. Surely she must have felt little reason to fight the dreaded effects of yellow fever. Ironically, another article written a short time later informed its readers that New Orleans had cleaned up their river and mosquito problem. The last stronghold of yellow fever faded into history, along with poor Beth."

It was too quiet. I turned to find Bree sitting in a chair, looking very pale.

"The cemetery. I know where it is."

"You're not serious, Bree! You don't really want to go to that cemetery!"

"We've come this far, Meredith. We might as well follow this story to its conclusion. It's in the center of the town."

We put things back as they had been found and went to find Mrs. Grenling. "We'll be leaving now, Mrs. Grenling; but before we go, I wonder if you could answer a couple of questions."

"I will do my best, Professor Evans."

"The cemetery used in the nineteenth century, could you tell me where it's located?"

"Oh, that's easy. Just follow Main Street to the center of town. You will run right into it. It's one of our historical sights."

"Thank you. Also, do you know anything about arsenic being used as medication in the late nineteenth century?"

"Yes, in fact I do. Because it caused symptoms which the Victorians felt to be signs of health, it was used as a medicine, smoked in a tobacco, and used cosmetically. They thought it would ward off consumption and cure other ailments. It gave people a robust glowing appearance and often caused them to gain weight. It was readily available in pharmacies in the form of tonics and pills and could be mixed with tobacco, along with other dangerous ingredients such as opium, cocaine, and alcohol. It's hard to imagine how many fell victim to these panaceas and the advice of Victorian physicians."

"Indeed! Thank you again, Mrs. Grenling."

We found the cemetery, just as Bree saw it, in the center of the town surrounded by stone walls. Under other circumstances, the cemetery alone would have been an historical find. Ornate marble decorating the graves was a magnificent tribute to a time when overdone was the fashion statement of the day.

The cemetery was small and well kept, with a lovely parklike atmosphere. Bree seemed to walk with purpose, having quickly left the car just as I pulled to the curb. We followed close behind her as she walked up to a statue of an angel done in white marble. The headstone at the feet of the angel read: "Our beloved son, Christopher Allen Tait, Born 1870, Died 1895. The Dear Child God has given us, He calls Home."

Beside his was Beth's grave. The marker read: "Elizabeth Alice Sterling, Born 1877, Died 1905. Our Elizabeth, no other could have been more loved as a daughter."

Bree sat on the wrought iron bench beside the graves looking rather distant. "It feels awfully strange to be looking at my own grave."

Meredith sat beside her, putting her arm around Bree and whispering gently to her. "It's a miracle of life that we live, Bree; that we move through lifetimes and emerge still alive, but better for the experience. Always remember that miracle, Bree. Always cherish that miracle."

"Then Christopher is somewhere, isn't he?"

"Of course, he must be somewhere, Bree."

"Here? Here in this time period with me?"

"I don't know. It's certainly possible, but . . . I don't know."

Bree looked exhausted. It was obvious she could use a rest and so we returned her home.

Meredith and I were off on another adventure. Could we find the current incarnated Christopher Tait? Did he exist in this time? What became of the spirit that lived in Victorian America, his happy life abruptly ended, over one hundred years ago? It seemed unreasonable that Bree would have so much recollection for no reason. Both Meredith and I understood that what we referred to as past life was of no consequence in the present. The fact that it could be traced was of some use to those who needed proof of continuing existence; but beside that, there was no value in having past life recall. It would only confuse and slow one's progress. We would be daunted by our dark and oppressive experiences and overly infatuated with our achievements. Too confusing and too tempting to remain so focused, contemplating what we have been. Surely, we all have done things in this lifetime that we would like to change. Can you imagine being inundated with data from other lifetimes, trying to resolve problems not currently affecting you? And we both understood that when one does have concrete recollection, as Bree was experiencing, it was for a reason. Some problem that occurred in her past life was affecting her present incarnation. Perhaps it was a problem that could be solved.

"It could be as simple as letting go subconsciously so that she can get on with forming present relationships. It might have nothing to do with finding Christopher Tait."

"Then why are all three of us so obsessed with finding him? I don't think that's it, Meredith. I think there's more to it. Why experience all this recollection and all this pain if for no other reason than to move her focus into her present life? We all incarnate into different situations. No, it's more than just accepting change. Something must be examined or found or completed. Something, but what?"

"And how do we go about finding him?"

"What did you say?"

"Hmmm?"

"You said, 'How do we go about finding him?' He is here, isn't he?"

"Yes . . ." Meredith spoke hesitantly. "Yes, I honestly believe he is."

"So, how do we find him?"

"It would be a simple process in the astral state. But he may have no experience with that reality and view us as simply an intruding dream. Then, trying to convince him we are real could take months!"

"There has to be a better way."

"There is, but we need someone with greater abilities than my own." Meredith's expression suddenly brightened. "And I believe I know just the person who can help us!"

We contacted Mrs. Grenling and requested copies of the wedding announcement and photograph of Beth and Christopher. After having received that, Meredith called upon a sage old teacher she had met since we moved here.

The opportunity to meet Jerry was the delight of my life. Meredith had made arrangements for us to go to his home. We made the trip one day after my last class.

Just outside Calvert was a densely wooded area. It was the same woods the little girl followed her cat into. I parked the car and followed Meredith into the woods and down several paths.

"I didn't know you were the outdoor type, Meredith!" We were both struggling to get through overgrown foliage. Meredith comically tried to keep from stepping into small holes made by tiny animals. My feet were too big so I was free to walk with no special precaution.

"I'm not, but this is where Jerry lives. The only time he leaves here is to visit the hospice in the neighboring town."

We came upon a modest cottage in the middle of the woods and knocked on the door. The door was opened by a fragile old man. He was small, slightly stooped, wearing a yellow satin gown loosely over thin pants and a pair of sandals.

"Jerry, this is Professor Evans."

"Lang, please." I took this frail old man's hand. To my surprise, the energy in that handshake was tremendous. And the look of love in his eyes was like nothing I have ever seen. He spoke English beautifully, with a slight lyrical eastern Indian accent.

"Please, won't you come inside."

We walked into a modest room. That was all it was, a room. A desk and a few chairs, a fireplace, and some cooking utensils. The fact that there was no bed struck me as odd. I wondered where this old man slept. Certainly not in a chair. But it seemed an intrusion of his privacy to ask.

"My American friends call me Jerry. My real name is in Sanskrit and does not translate. It is too difficult for them to pronounce and seeing it written in its original Sanskrit is too confusing. Jerry is close enough and easy to remember! I do not often have company, but I made some tea in anticipation of your visit. Won't you join me?"

"Are you a monk, Jerry?"

"That was my training among the masters in the Himalayan mountains of India, my homeland. But my work is here."

"And what is it you do?"

"I teach the dying to release their spirits, giving them comfort. I answer their questions about what to expect when the time comes for them to leave us. When they successfully release their spirit, they do not feel the pain of the dying body, and often their fear leaves them as well."

"Meredith told me your work takes you to a hospice?"

"For the same purpose, yes. Hospice, hospitals, homes, wherever I am needed to help a soul about to experience a transition. Meredith has told me of your classes at the university, Lang. I am always delighted to meet those who teach the truth. In this time, it is needed more than it ever has been. Now it can be understood by so many who need its nurturance. But, what can I do for you today?"

We explained the experiences beginning with Bree's search for a past life and ending with the information we found in Downer Woods.

"I feel as though there is a reason for all of this to surface in Bree's life. The time and place, none of this is coincidental."

"You are right, of course, Meredith. Coincidence is a meaningless word used to excuse man's ignorance of his own environment. Have you brought me anything that would put me in touch with the energy of these souls?"

"Yes, Jerry." Meredith produced a current photograph of Bree, and also the copy of the wedding announcement photo of Beth and Christopher.

"Such sadness for this young woman. She has experienced much loss in this life, also."

There seemed no need to respond.

"The young man lives again, and they are destined to meet, but they keep missing each other." Jerry was amused by this thought. "I see them in a great hall and just about the time they should have met, one or the other was removed from the meeting place. But you are correct; they have unfinished business. I need to begin a meditation to align with this spirit. It is your intention to find him, is it not?"

"Yes, Jerry. Like you, we feel these two have unfinished business."

"They learn and grow well in each other's company. If you will, meditate with me, please?"

The power in this room could generate enough energy to light a city. It was a privilege to meditate in the company of this soft-spoken, yet wise man. We meditated for one hour; but it seemed like the time a flame takes to flicker. In all my years experiencing this ancient practice, I never remembered experiencing the passage of time at what seemed light speed.

Glowing and refreshed as we all were, Jerry opened his eyes with renewed exhilaration. His appearance was somehow more youthful, softer. His eyes fell on the photographs we had provided and he spoke.

"He is an architect, once again. There is a great love of that art that he was not given the time to fulfill in his last experience. And he loves to work with historical buildings, again honoring the century he left prematurely. Oh, very amusing!"

"What is amusing, Jerry?"

"He was born to the very same family. The man you are looking for is Christopher Allen Tait! These people are a close group. He came back as the grandson of his own brother. Obviously he had no intention of prematurely dying as the original Christopher Tait. Just some bad health choices, I suspect. He will be at the campus where you teach, Lang, to design an addition for your Fine

Arts building, specifically the auditorium. I am certain you will be told of his arrival if you inquire about the addition. Look for him in one week. Your friend is fortunate to have you as guides. You look on her as a daughter, don't you? Did you know you were her parents in that period of the nineteenth century?"

"Parents?" We both responded at once, stunned!

"Yellow fever. Such a terrible disease in its time. It took both of you at once, almost instantly. There was no time before your passing for you to prepare her. You had planned so much to teach her. You watched over her after your crossing, but it wasn't the same.

And when her Christopher passed on, you wept alongside of her. She did not know, but you were there, one on each side to give her strength. And so you are all here, together again. The miracle of rebirth! But this time, you will influence this soul as you had first intended. Energy never dies, children. Love never dies."

We were speechless! I had never come across this life in the nineteenth century, and neither had Meredith. But we instinctively knew that what Jerry saw was accurate. We did treat Bree as though she were our daughter. We fussed over her and made her happiness a priority between us. Surely we continued our parenting in this life with Bree.

I was so fascinated by this man who sat before me, I threw decorum to the wind and asked the question that plagued my thoughts.

"Forgive me for prying, Jerry. But I have to ask. Why . . ." He answered before I could finish the question.

"Because I do not sleep. There is no bed because I do not sleep. That was your question, was it not?"

I could only nod and Jerry continued his explanation. "I do not sleep because my affiliation with this realm and this physical body is a temporary one used only to bring comfort to those who could not receive me were I in another form."

"You mean in spirit."

"Yes. This body is older than you can imagine. I was not born to it, not in the sense that you would associate birth."

"Not born to it?" Today, I was the student.

"That is right. My advancement was such that to suffer the trauma of birth and growth would have been a waste of my time. The experience had nothing to teach me. Yet I needed to have access to the physical world and those in it. And so, an old monk whose work was nearly done was feeling the weariness of his age. The time was drawing near for him to move to a new level. He graciously relinquished his body to me when he was ready to leave it. With his blessing, I took over the functioning of this physical manifestation. I completed his chosen work as a monk, fulfilling his few final wishes, and then devoted myself to my own. But it is not necessary for me to remain in it for long periods of time as humans do, burrowing into the physical world as a butterfly not ready to emerge from a cocoon."

"So, essentially, you leave your body and live in another dimension, as you teach the dying to do."

"That is correct. It aids me in my work. Once they have learned to release their spirits, aren't they amused to find me standing beside them!" Jerry chuckled at the prospect of a spirit finding him in the state they progressed to in an attempt to avoid the pain of a dying body. I was delighted with his infectious sense of humor. In his loving, giving way, with a twinkling merriment, he taught the continuation of life and abolished the fear of death, standing beside his patients at each stage of their journey.

"It must surprise them, but it must also comfort them."

"And, of course, that is why I am here."

I am forever grateful to the powers of the universe when I am able to meet one such as Jerry. I cannot begin to describe the sheer joy of being in the company of a soul with that much wisdom. And wisdom accompanies love, it is almost inseparable. Being in their company, they lavish you generously with their limitless energy. A buoyancy seems to overtake you. You have to suppress the urge to laugh and cry out with joy and celebration. It gives credence to my work and refills the power and joy in its continuation.

"So . . . we were married!" It was an intense conversation for the ride home.

"Is that so hard to believe, Lang?"

"Well, no. I mean, I could see us married. But if we were married in a previous life, what has kept us from marrying in this one?"

"Is that a proposal?"

"No!"

"Well, you don't have to be that adamant about it!"

I took on a gentler tone. "No, I mean . . . I just can't see myself married. It never seemed on the agenda. But of course, if I were to marry, well . . . of course, it would be you!"

"If that's a compliment, thanks! But what makes you think I would accept?"

"You wouldn't?"

"I didn't say that."

"Then you would?"

"That brings us back to my first question. Is this a proposal?"

"You don't want to be married to me, Meredith."

"Your intuition is right on, Lang!"

"What?"

"You would make me live in places where I could die of dreaded diseases! Some husband you made!"

"Well . . . I would try harder this time!"

Meredith hit me in the arm with her purse. "No one in this car is getting married. That's all I need in my life, a stuffy overbearing professor for a husband! Besides, it's Bree's love life we are trying to jump start, not ours."

"That's right. Of course, you're right." I looked over at Meredith, obviously distressed with this topic, and gave her a knowing grin. "I think we just never felt marriage was an option for either of us. We don't need to embellish what we already have, do we?"

"Do you know what I think?"

"What, Meredith?"

"I think we should change the subject while we're still friends!"

I reached over and squeezed her hand as we laughed, happy just to be in each other's company.

# Chapter 12

Monday morning found me in President Stepton's office enjoying a pre-class conversation and some of his wonderful specially brewed coffee.

"Is there truth to the rumor that we are to have an addition built on to the Fine Arts building, Martin?"

"News certainly travels fast around this campus, Lang. How did you find out? I thought I had kept that secret quite well. You didn't pick this up by psychic means, did you?"

It took some fast thinking to keep my cover. I chose to give him a moment before responding and let him arrive at his own conclusion. "Well, not completely. But it's a fine idea. We have such a wonderful theater group. We could use a larger stage and extra seating. It must be difficult to find an architect versed in the Gothic style. Whom did you unearth, Martin; and when will we meet him?"

"We were so fortunate, Lang. Mr. Tait showed up in my office, right off the street, hoping to become involved in expanding the building!"

"Did he really?"

"Yes! He told me he had been to several performances and enjoyed them. But, like you, he felt the facility was lacking in size and that we could attract a far larger crowd of theater-goers if only we had more space. The Fine Arts Department had been requesting an expansion for years and we should have done it by now. But finding the right architect . . . We just didn't want to entrust such a project to the wrong firm. Tait and Sons has been in business since the nineteenth century."

"Is that right?" Shivers crept down my back at the sound of 'Tait and Sons'."

"Yes. Their specialty was Gothic and Victorian architecture. Chris, that is, Mr. Tait, has made quite a study of that period. If I didn't know better, I would say he lived then. Wait until you meet him, Lang. You won't believe it. He even looks Victorian."

I was experiencing a relentless case of the chills listening to Martin describe Chris's Victorian demeanor. "I would like to see this walking anachronism for myself, Martin. If he's half as Victorian as Bree . . . I have a great idea! Since he loves Victorian architecture, I am certain I could convince Bree to host a small dinner party in her home. I think Chris would be delighted with what he would find there." Sometimes, I can't believe how deceitful I can be. Well, it's all for a good cause.

"I have an appointment with him this afternoon. I will talk to him about dinner and let you know when he's free."

And it was arranged. Meredith suggested we not inform Bree prior to their meeting. Instead we prevailed on her good nature to host a small but important dinner party. We wanted this to proceed without any more interference. The night chosen was clear and crisp. Winter was a gentler season that year, and it was close to Christmas. There was something in the air: romance, festivity, even the mansion looked to be dressed in party best. Bree had seen to every detail. The menu was planned to entice all guests.

The house was decorated for Christmas with exquisite Victorian ornamentation. And my favorite piece, the dining room chandelier, was lit with soft pink bulbs casting an ethereal glow. Bree was dressing upstairs as Meredith and I walked around the first floor. Cook gave us first taste on some wonderful dishes, and the house felt warm and inviting.

"They will meet in half an hour. What do you think? Is this as magical as it feels?"

"I have such a wonderful feeling about tonight, Lang. It's as though Cinderella were upstairs getting ready to meet her prince!"

"Should we have told her?"

"And ruin the surprise? Of course not! Bree will talk of this meeting years from now; it may be a story she will tell her grandchildren." Meredith dried an escaping tear as it made its way down her cheek. I gave her a hug and she seemed to melt a little in my arms. "It does feel as though we are Bree's family, doesn't it."

"She could do worse."

"True. And I could do worse than have someone as wonderful as you in my life."

The door chimed its announcement of impending guests. Chimes melodically rivaling the bells of a cathedral added to the romance of this night. We opened the door to find Martin and a tall young gentleman standing behind him. Christopher had dark curly hair, green eyes and a charming smile. His resemblance to the gentleman in the engagement photo was remarkable. I wondered if Bree would recognize him. He had dressed impeccably and as he reached over to extend his hand, I sensed a knowing, worldly spirit within him. "It's a pleasure to meet you, Mr. Tait. Won't you please come in?"

"Thank you; but please, call me Chris."

"The lady of the house is upstairs. Meredith, would you like to tell Bree her guests have arrived?"

Meredith seemed to be in a trance. "Meredith?"

"What? Oh! Yes, Bree! Certainly, I will get her." She nearly sprinted up the staircase. Moments later, we watched two feminine visions descending the stairs. Bree was more beautiful than I had ever seen her. I was certain that Meredith had given her some hint about the importance of her dinner guest. She wore a champagne-colored dress that seemed to add a light and sparkle to her beautiful auburn hair. We watched the expressions of this young couple as they greeted each other for the first time in one hundred years! Chris could not take his eyes off of Bree; and Bree had a knowing look. I assumed she recognized her long-lost love instantly.

"If you would excuse me, please. I must check with Cook. Meredith could you come with me? And Lang, please, if you would show our guests into the great hall." They left the foyer, Bree escorting Meredith very deliberately toward the kitchen, holding her arm. Max came into the great hall to take orders for drinks and, not wanting to miss the festivities, I quietly excused myself. In the kitchen, I came upon an excited discussion. Bree turned and looked at me. "How did you find him?"

"She knows?"

"The minute she saw his face, Lang."

"Well, there's no time to explain that now. Just reintroduce yourself to your soul mate, and enjoy this evening. Go on, now!"

"What's his last name?"

"Tait."

"What? You're joking!"

"No. We will explain all this later. You have dinner guests. Now compose yourself and get in there!" Meredith adopted the role of "mother" with ease. I couldn't help myself and gave her a wink from behind Bree's back. Ever the dutiful "daughter" Bree turned on one heel and left the kitchen.

"You handled her well, Mother!"

"Oh! You get in there, too! And stop enjoying this so much!"

We followed Bree into the great hall where she announced to her guests that dinner was being served in the dining room. Glorious as usual, the table was set with everything imaginable.

"Bree, you have outdone yourself tonight."

"Yes, Bree, thank you so much for having this little party." Martin Stepton, unaware of anything but a wonderful meal, looked especially pleased with the feast that was laid before him.

"It's my pleasure, Martin. I so rarely entertain here; I am delighted for the opportunity."

"That's truly a shame, Ms. Lambeau. This house should be alive with guests and music as often as possible." Chris's melodious rich speaking voice had Bree in a trance. "These homes were built to entertain. It is the house's legacy."

"You know, you're right, Chris. But please, call me Bree. I promise I will make an effort to do more entertaining if I can be assured of your attendance?" Bree was certainly not lacking in charm. "Have you started the plans for the new Fine Arts addition?"

"In fact, I have several drawings ready. I would like to share them with you first. You pick your favorites and those will be the ones I present to the committee. May I so boldly elicit your help, Bree?"

She was caught, once again, by this handsome Victorian. The man she loved as the young Beth was now returned to her. Meredith smiled as we both acknowledged the look on Bree's face.

Chris was more than a potential mate, he was her life. A life cut short by a premature death in the late flower of the nineteenth century, then reunited to assist each other through the latter part of the twentieth century.

And this young woman deserved such happiness. Lost in the reverie of this potential romance, I missed Bree's response to Chris's question. But from the look on Chris's face, it was apparent she had agreed to assist him in choosing the best plans for the Fine Arts building addition.

They watched each other as though they were the only two in the room. We might have arranged for them to meet alone; however, we felt there would be many more meetings for them. Why not share in this romantic reunion? After all, this was the culmination of Meredith's and my work. We deserved to witness their first meeting. It was a joyous occasion to see Bree, in bloom as one of her many exquisite garden flowers, as we had never seen her before.

Hours passed as we lingered over dinner, then cordials back in the great hall. Chris asked Bree if he might see the rest of the mansion. It was their opportunity to get away together. They returned twenty minutes later.

"This home is magnificent. Every detail has been lovingly restored. It's as though it had been built last week."

"I am happy you like it, Chris."

Martin broke the reverie with a dose of reality. "Oh my, look at the time! You have an early class tomorrow, and I have early appointments. We have to end this evening. Bree, thank you so much for your wonderful hospitality. And please, send along my appreciation to your kitchen staff. They prepared a splendid meal."

"I will tell them, Martin. As Chris pointed out earlier, we should be entertaining more in the mansion. It will not be long before you are invited back again."

"I look forward to it, my dear."

"May we get together and go over those plans some time tomorrow, Bree?"

"Yes, Chris, give me a call and let me know what time would be convenient for you."

"Well, I thought I might pick you up around eight and take you to dinner."

"How nice. Yes, please; I accept."

The formalities of showing guests to the door over, Bree turned to her sources for information. "You two aren't going anywhere!"

Meredith couldn't resist the opportunity to tease her. "Really, Dear, it is late!"

"Oh no! Just make yourselves comfortable and start with telling me how you found him, and why he has the same name!"

"Well, if you insist. You remember Jerry, Bree?"

"The Indian man who wandered into the counseling center a few months ago? Yes, I do. He's so wonderful, but what does he have to do with this?"

"Well, he cut a lot of red tape and told us that the two of you were destined to meet again. According to Jerry, the two of you should have met at some function in a ballroom. He said as you were about to be introduced, one of you was called away."

"Ballroom? Why, yes, I remember! Three years ago, I was invited to a charity ball given by the Society for Historical Restoration. They needed funds to save a beautiful old home that had been turned into a museum. The event was held in the ballroom. I remember I was about to be introduced to the architect who fought so hard to keep the building from being destroyed. The city wanted to put a parking lot there, and their argument was that restoration and maintenance required an astronomical sum. The architect donated his time to the project to help cut costs and I was anxious to meet him. We had cocktails before dinner, and a friend of my father's offered to introduce me to him. The ballroom held as many people as its capacity would allow. We had to make an effort to get through a crowd of people. As we approached, a woman crossed in front of us and he was whisked out of the room! I didn't even get a look at his face!"

"Clearly, you would have met anyway, without our help. You are so involved with the university, I know you would have been introduced to him at some point. We just couldn't resist assisting. After all, we had come this far!"

"I am so happy you did. Both of you do so much for me. I don't know how I will ever repay you."

"We are family, Bree. No one is keeping track of favors."

"But how do you explain the name?"

"Professor, you're on!" Meredith playfully winked at me.

"We sometimes become so attached to people, forming relationships incarnation after incarnation, that we choose to come back together. Usually in different roles, but the familiarity of having loved ones in our lives one incarnation to the next is a comforting one.

Apparently, the original Christopher Tait passed on prematurely. He then chose to become the grandchild of his own brother, who named him after the brother who was so suddenly lost to the family. Although he was not consciously aware that this was the same spirit, it wouldn't surprise me to discover that he had some subconscious awareness of the lineage of his new grandchild. And, although Christopher is not consciously aware of it, he came back to find you, as well."

"Oh my! Forgive me, please!" Bree shyly looked away, embarrassed by her tearful response.

"You deserve happiness in your life, Bree. You have done so much for others. See that you enjoy every minute of this reunion."

"Yes, Meredith, thank you. I will. Thank you. Thank you both!" Bree sat between us and put her arms around us for a hug.

✒

And now, I must stop to address your questions. You, the reader, as much my student as those who come daily to the university. You have questions. No, you have doubts. Doubts of what you are reading.

How can there be so many happy endings? How can all of these situations end so perfectly as though they were orchestrated by some genius? You want to believe in happy endings, but your life has proven conclusively that there is no such thing. That no matter what your chosen path, you will falter and ultimately fail. You may believe you must settle for whatever keeps you safe.

Is it a job you are not fond of? Do you go to a place every day doing far less than you know you are capable of? Why? Is it because you know that job is something you can count on? Are you afraid to try what you know deep inside you would fulfill you? Do you fear stepping beyond your self-inflicted boundaries? Yes, I did say self inflicted. And if you should try and fail, what then? You will have lost the security of the job that has kept food on your table, a roof over your head. Or, from a different point of longing, the relationship you want so desperately constantly eludes you. You always seem to attract the person who is wrong for you.

When you think of what you want, you think of these things in terms of despair. You feel the void of not having. The thought brings tears to your eyes and a heaviness to your heart. Isn't that how it feels? If you come away from this reading with only one lesson, let it be this: You are a creator. The power that created you did so in and of itself.

You came into this lifetime, this environment, to experience the joy and beauty of a physical world. But, instead of using that ability to create the joyousness that is your birthright, you create out of those feelings of lack, attracting more of what you don't want, and little of what you do.

Consider feeling for what it truly is, a gauge or barometer of that which you are currently creating and drawing into your personal experience. Understand that your negative emotions are a warning system, telling you that you are about to bring more of what you don't want into your life. Knowing that, change those feelings to joyful ones. See the situation as exhilarating and fulfilling just the way you truly want it. Do this habitually and watch your life change. Having offered the advice I believe will most benefit you, let us return to our story.

✗o

We had to tell him. The students, especially the Angels were exchanging ideas and hypotheses about the true identity of the man whose name was forever engraved in their minds. It was obvious there was no coincidence here. It would soon be blurted out to him, unwittingly, that not coincidentally, a man with the very same name and profession as Chris was in a past incarnation with Gabrielle Lambeau. That would be disastrous. Chris had to hear the truth from us, from Bree. But, of course, Bree was apprehensive. How would he respond? What would he do? To this point, Chris tolerated the psychic world because Bree, the woman he loved so dearly, insisted he accept it as a valid possibility. How would he respond to knowing he lived before, knowing he had left Bree over one hundred years prior, in a time when single women were emotionally incomplete? Meredith just shook her head.

"I know we have to tell him, but I don't have the slightest idea how he will react. I care too much about their happiness. I just can't tune in. I say do it and get it over with. We have no choice. We will deal with his reaction when we are confronted with it."

Over dinner in the mansion, Bree, Chris, Meredith, and I sat silently, no one wanting to begin.

"Why is everyone so quiet tonight? Usually you are talking over each other. What in heaven's name is going on?" To Chris, our silence was deafening.

"Chris, there is something you don't know, and we want to tell you before you hear it from someone else."

"What, Bree? Why do you look so serious? Is someone sick?"

"No, no, it's nothing like that." Meredith, trying to make Chris more at ease, allayed his worst fear.

"Well, what then? Don't tell me, the board is dissatisfied with the Fine Arts building."

"No, that's not it, either, Chris. Your ideas were wonderful and the work is being impeccably done. Everyone is enchanted with the plans and the progress." Bree's sincerity was clear.

"It's something we know that you do not. And the worst part is that you are not at all prepared for what you are about to find out. It's nothing you won't be able to live with, but it may be something you will find difficult to accept."

"Bree. You're nervous and you're rambling. Obviously it is very important. You all look so serious. Professor Evans?"

"It is important. But it may come as quite a shock to you. We wanted to do this as gently as possible." Both Bree and Meredith were giving me those pleading looks that told me they wanted me to continue. "I guess I've been elected, so I'll start. Some time ago, before you undertook the Fine Arts building addition, we did, oh, what would you call it . . . an experiment."

"An experiment?"

"That's right. Bree volunteered to be put under hypnosis to demonstrate past life regression." I thought I should stop there a moment and let this young man digest what I had said. The growing look of concern on his face told me we were sailing over rough water on a less-than-suitable vessel.

"You mean Bree has lived before?" Chris was becoming noticeably uncomfortable.

"We would not be telling you this, Chris, except for the fact that the experiment was done in front of literally hundreds of students and faculty. You are going to have to understand what occurred since it won't be long before someone begins to put some puzzle pieces together. That is assuming they have not already done so. Bree experienced a lifetime in the late nineteenth century. She was engaged to be married to a fine young man, who unfortunately, with improper medical advice, passed on prematurely. This young man was an architect. We think we have concrete, indisputable evidence, Chris, that you were that young man."

No one said a word. Chris sat speechless for what seemed like an eternity. "I don't want to insult you, Professor, but I don't believe in reincarnation."

"Oh, you will, Chris, you will."

"Excuse me?"

"It came as a shock to me, too, Chris. Certainly, I have good reason to believe in reincarnation. But the entire ordeal made it a striking reality with real people and tense situations."

Chris looked over at Bree, a pleading look, seeking an ally. "Bree, you are one of the most intelligent, sensitive young women I know. Couldn't all of this just be some sort of wishful thinking? Some kind of fantasy? I mean, reincarnation, Bree, really."

"No, Chris. When Lang tells you he has indisputable evidence, that is just what he has. He is, after all, a scientist, one of the most respected in his field."

"Well, yes, of course. I didn't mean to diminish your credibility, Professor. But reincarnation? Me?"

Meredith was sensing Chris's growing agitation. "Would you like to continue this at another time, Chris? Maybe you would like to do a little research of your own on the subject before we continue with this conversation."

"No, Meredith. I want to see what you have. I want to see this proof."

They all turned and looked at me. If I ever wanted to be somewhere else, this was the time. "I have to first tell you that I do not encourage people to explore their incarnations. It's just not a necessary thing unless there is some spillover, if you will, from one life to another. And certainly, in your case, except for extenuating circumstances, we would not be having this conversation. But people sometimes feel the need to remain with those with whom they are familiar from one incarnation to the next. You did that, Chris."

"I did?"

"In a rather creative way, in fact. As I said before, you died prematurely, and as far as we can tell, came back to continue your life with Bree, and exercise your marvelous talents in the field of architecture. Specifically, Victorian architecture."

This last comment made Chris twist uncomfortably in his chair. "O.K., I admit a fondness for Victorian architecture, but that doesn't prove I lived in the nineteenth century!"

"In 1895, at the age of eighteen, a young woman named Beth Sterling became engaged to a gentleman, seven years her senior. This young man was a very talented architect who had recently joined his family's firm."

"But what makes you think I was this man?"

"The firm was the finest in Chicago. It originated in Downer Woods. It was the firm of Tait and Sons. The young man's name was Christopher Allen Tait."

"Now, wait a minute! My great uncle, for whom I was named, was Christopher Allen Tait."

"That's right, and he . . . that is, you, died in 1895."

"What? This is insane! So you found evidence of my great uncle's profession and his death. Really, Professor, that's hardly conclusive! It's ludicrous! How could I have been my own great uncle?"

"We have reason to believe that is just who you were. We have a photograph you will find very interesting. There's more. You were born to this family again to fulfill the life you left prematurely. When you came to this door for the first time, Bree recognized you instantly. You might see why." With that I handed him the engagement photo of Beth and Christopher.

"He died young, and I've always been told I look like him. It's just a coincidence, Professor, really!" His gaze then rested on the picture of Beth standing beside her intended. "It is you. Your hair is different, but it's you." Bree took Chris's hand to offer support.

"That's right, Chris. Under hypnosis, Beth was able to tell all about her engagement to you. She also informed us of your name and how you died so tragically on your wedding day. The day after the session, the three of us went to Downer Woods to try to verify what Beth had told us under hypnosis. We found everything to be exactly as she informed us. Because of the accuracy of her recollection under hypnosis, we were able to verify all this information.

For example, your father, Alphonse, died of consumption. Because of an overpowering fear of experiencing such a death, you sought the advice of a physician. The so-called medication he suggested you use to ward off consumption actually was your undoing. While we were there, Bree was able to lead us to the cemetery and the plots where both Christopher and Beth were buried. Christopher died in 1895. Beth died of yellow fever in 1905, as her parents had. The families apparently wanted the young couple to be together symbolically in death, since they were both lost to them. Christopher and Beth were buried side by side, instead of in respective family plots."

"This is the truth, Bree? You saw this lifetime while you were under hypnosis?"

"Yes, Chris, it's the truth."

"We knew we had to find you, and sought the help of a highly gifted friend who informed us that you had incarnated into the same family and had the same name. Unwittingly, you were also looking for Bree. You had already made plans to do the architectural work on the university's Fine Arts building. So finding you was incredibly easy."

"I was determined to work on that building, even if I had to waive my entire fee just to get that job."

"Well, I wouldn't announce that to President Stepton!" Meredith, trying to be somewhat jovial, made a vain attempt to lighten the mood.

"According to the gentleman who helped us locate you, the two of you should have met at a party in a ballroom, but one of you was whisked away before the meeting could take place."

"It was the fund-raising party for the restoration of the beer baron's mansion in the city of Clear River." Bree offered this information bringing a concrete image for Christopher to hold on to.

"You were there?"

"Yes, I tried to meet you, but . . ."

"There was such a crowd that night."

"That's right. I couldn't even get a look at your face. I was about three people away from you when someone pushed her way through the crowd and whisked you off."

"Reincarnation. I don't know what to think. Surely you would not be making all of this up."

"We would have no reason to do that, Chris."

"No, of course, I know. I have to think about this. Bree, I know we made plans for this weekend, but I have to go away. I need some time to think."

"Whatever you need to do, Chris. I understand."

"You might want to take this with you, Chris."

"What is on this tape, Professor?"

"That is the taped session of Bree's recollection of past life while under hypnosis. When you listen to it, it may stir some past life memory. I do hope you will avail yourself of Meredith's or my help in trying to cope with what you are discovering. We are not taking any of this lightly and realize fully how disconcerting this must be for you."

"I appreciate that, Professor. And I know where to find you both. Thank you."

We finished dinner rather uncomfortably. The next morning Bree phoned Meredith to tell her that Chris had left his apartment with no information on when or if he would be returning.

"Just give him some time, Bree. You have to trust him to do what is right. We gave him a large dose of information to digest at supper last night. He's in a state of shock. After all, he was totally unprepared for any of this. It couldn't be helped, but I would have preferred more time. Unfortunately, time was something we could not afford to waste. He needs to take some time now. He has a lot to think about. Whatever spirituality he was comfortable with, we have no doubt given him serious reason to re-evaluate his beliefs."

"I am so afraid he will not handle this well, and I will lose him again."

"Now, don't give in to an anxiety attack, Bree. Everything will work out fine. You will see."

It was a long week. As the days went by, Bree seemed to be slipping. She looked resigned, depressed, and was reclusive. Nothing we could tell her seemed to help. Finally, the following

Saturday we forced Bree out of her house and took her on a long drive through Calvert's splendid countryside. We enjoyed snow-blanketed scenery, icicle-trimmed trees, and crisp winter air, then had lunch at a charming roadside inn before the return ride to Calvert. As we walked to the doorway of the mansion, Bree turned and hugged us both. Sensing something had changed, we were not about to leave. Bree opened the front door to find the contents of at least two florist shops in the foyer."

"Oh my word! Look at all these flowers!"

A note tucked into a bouquet of two dozen pink roses read: "You won't be so easily rid of me in this life. I intend to be with you for many years to come. Love, Chris."

As she dried her tears and looked up, Chris walked out of the great hall with open arms.

"I think we can leave now, Lang."

"You are an astute psychic, Meredith!"

As if informing Chris of his Victorian incarnation wasn't enough, the students were about to create an uprising. I could no longer contain all of their questions, and decided that fielding them as they came up was the best, least conspicuous way. Slowly, as unceremoniously as possible, Chris was introduced to the students as the one and only Christopher Allen Tait, survivor from the nineteenth century and proof of life after life.

He was so good-natured considering people were prying into his very sensitive distant past, a past he had yet to come to terms with. He went to pick Bree up for dinner one evening at the counseling center, and was confronted by the Angels. As I walked in the door, it became obvious the man had been cornered. They were not about to let him leave before they had some questions answered. Alex was firing questions in rapid succession.

"Did you change your major, Alex? Plan to become a reporter? A lawyer, maybe?"

"No, Professor, but I think Mr. Tait should introduce himself to everyone who heard about his previous life. After all we . . ."

"After all, Alex, really! The sensitivity of this issue and the privacy of Mr. Tait, who was completely unaware of his past life, let alone its display before nearly the entire student body at Fields, should be our priority. Not rampant curiosity."

"I don't mind questions, Professor."

"That's a generous attitude, Chris. But you might want to ponder the reciprocal nature of that statement before you commit to it. How much of this do you really want revealed? When I explained to the students that we would return with the results of the research verifying Bree's past life recall, I had no idea I would be involving an innocent party. You were told of past life, yours, a shock in itself. Then to be confronted with a mob of curious students and its pack leader, Alex! Alex, you ought to be ashamed."

"I am sorry, Professor. I thought . . ."

"You didn't think, that's the trouble."

"It's all right, I understand everyone's curiosity. I think right now I would just like to take Bree to dinner. Maybe she could help me sort this out and we will get back to you."

"Certainly, Chris. Have a good dinner and a good talk."

As if on cue, Bree walked out of her office and joined us. "My two favorite gentlemen, what a nice surprise. Will you be joining us for dinner, Lang?"

"No, Bree. I think the two of you have a rather important issue to discuss. Let me know what you decide, Chris."

Later that evening, I was reading in my living room near a warm fire. I glanced at my watch, 9 P.M., just as the doorbell rang. Within moments, I was ushering Chris in from the cold.

"Bree did not come with you?"

"No, Professor. She was rather tired and I took her home."

"I see. Please make yourself comfortable. Would you like a hot cup of coffee?"

"If it's no trouble."

"No, I have a pot here. Was Bree able to help with your problem?"

"Yes. Bree is not at all shy about her incarnation as Beth. She pointed out to me that the truth is far more important than her privacy in this matter. And although I became an innocent participant, well, in this life, at least, I am part of the adventure."

"A rather dramatic part, in fact."

"I think the truth must be told to the students, at least the ones who attended Bree's search for a past life."

"That would be quite a number. The theater was packed, with little standing room left. And those who did not attend have heard all about it, I can assure you. This was no quiet experiment."

"I intend to stay in Calvert, and I might as well face the music."

"You're planning to stay passed the renovation?"

"I've asked Bree to marry me."

"Yes, of course you have."

"You don't seemed surprised, Professor."

"I would have been more surprised if you had not. Well then, I agree; the sooner we answer all these questions the better. I have quietly been answering some of them for you, and reminding the students that your privacy is their utmost responsibility. Until tonight and Alex's uncontained enthusiastic inquisition, we had fared rather well. The truth is that at the time of the past life discovery, I had left the audience with a promise that we would fill them in on our factual search. We would be verifying facts told to us by Bree under hypnosis and we would report back to them."

"You had mentioned that earlier this evening. And Bree

brought up the promise, as well. Would the next session be held in the theater again?"

"Ideally, yes."

"Well, then I guess I had better plan on being part of the show."

"When do you anticipate completion of the renovation, Chris?"

"Another three weeks ought to be sufficient time. We are just about at the stage of final touches now. Some of the gilding to match the original decor may be completed after we reopen the theater. The university is anxious to have the theater operational again, and I assured Dr. Stepton that we would complete the major portion of the project, reopen the theater and continue with paint, etc., during hours it is not in use."

"Then we will announce an open meeting to be held in the theater to share gathered information on Bree's past life session in about three weeks?"

"Yes."

"You are comfortable with this?"

"Not completely, but for Bree's sake, yes."

"You're a brave soul, Chris. The concept takes some getting used to, but I think as you contemplate reincarnation as reality, you will find it becoming more logical an idea."

"You were right about the tape, Professor."

"Oh? In what way, Chris?"

"You said it might bring back distant memories. An image of an office Tait and Sons no longer occupies seemed to appear in my thoughts; and try as I might, I could not dispel it. I decided to do a little research on my own, looking through old family photographs. I found the exact office among my grandfather's photos. It gave me chills because the room was the same as the one I envisioned down to the smallest detail.

And the account of my father having died of consumption, I could feel the anxiety all over again. I simply knew it was the truth. To this day, I have this fear of the common cold, especially when it travels to the coughing stage. I seem to panic. I always had that reaction, and now I know why."

"Indeed! And now that you know why, you can expect that anxiety to be alleviated. That's one of the benefits of delving into one's past life."

"And, of course, Bree . . ."

"What about her, Chris?"

"From the moment I saw her, I felt so close to her. It was a feeling I couldn't understand. My career has always been my priority. I have dated, certainly, but never felt a need to find a permanent relationship. Bree is not just a charming woman, she seems somehow to be part of me."

"You're very fortunate to have this chance with her again."

"Yes, I think you are right. But reincarnation, it will take some time to get used to the idea."

"I suspect it might. Some time after your introduction, I suspect the curiosity will die down. Then I suggest you try to relax and enjoy your lives together. Don't become obsessed with what you have discovered. The fact that you have discovered a different incarnation is of little consequence in this life. It should not stand in the way of your happiness or fulfillment. You will feel more comfortable with the idea after you have learned a bit more about it. Then, put it aside and get on with things."

"The more I get to know you and Meredith, the more I understand Bree's love for the two of you."

"No you don't, Chris, but one shock at a time, my friend, one shock at a time!" Chris looked at me as though he were about to question that statement. Thoughts crossing his mind were revealed in his facial expression. He decided to leave well enough alone, and smiled pleasantly bidding me a good evening on his departure.

Busily attending classes, students, and the work of the Angels, time flew as usual. Meredith and I prepared a speech for the students who would come for the proof we had promised them. Bree's incarnation as Beth and of life after life. There was little point in trying to play down Chris's part in this dramatic scenario, even though both of us were intuitively aware of his need to stay out of the spotlight. But he bravely sat in the front row as we offered information to the students. The day had come.

"Ladies and Gentlemen, the most dramatic find in all of this experiment was Christopher Tait himself. You know him as the architect, the genius behind the restoration and addition to the building we are now occupying. Suffice it to say that this genius was cultivated in the state of Illinois over one hundred years ago." The crowd began to hum with excitement. "Much to his surprise, Chris has discovered his own past incarnation. He is here today and has graciously agreed to share this experience with all of you. Chris?"

Gulping a deep breath, Chris resolutely and speedily left his seat and climbed the five steps to the stage. He walked to my side and shook my hand. The audience applauded wildly, giving Chris a standing ovation.

"I really didn't do anything to deserve all this adulation. But I thank you."

"Chris, we have dramatically enlarged your engagement photo from 1895 to let the audience see it clearly. As we can all see, neither Chris nor Bree has changed much in appearance. But then, how does one improve on perfection? Bree, will you join us onstage?" Standing in front of a blown-up engagement photo from 1895, the resemblance was uncanny. We allowed the audience several minutes to examine the picture against its twentieth century counterpart and talk among themselves.

"Can we ask questions, Professor?" Alex could contain her curiosity no longer.

"Certainly, Alex. What do you want to know?"

"I want to know what it feels like. I mean, how do you feel knowing you lived . . . and died before?"

"May I answer that question, Professor?"

"Please, Chris."

Chris stepped up to the mike. "I can tell you that all of this came as quite a shock to me. I never even entertained the idea of reincarnation, let alone gave it serious thought. Then, almost overnight, I was caught up in a lead role in a confusing drama.

I spent so much of my life preparing for my career that I thought little of my own mortality. It was a subject I felt uncomfortable with, so I ignored it, as I am sure many do. Professor Evans gave me the tape of the hypnosis session to listen to privately. I was amazed, not only at what I heard on the tape, but of the feelings of recognition that were awakened in me. I could not dismiss what I was hearing as foolishness because I was instinctively aware that it was the truth.

How does it feel? It's frightening and invigorating all at the same time. It's frightening because of the mystery. It's invigorating because I know I can rectify any mistakes. Nothing can be permanently damaged, and knowing that gives me a hopeful feeling unlike anything I have ever experienced.

Professor Evans says that it's not necessary to explore one's past lives.

He feels that for the most part it is preferable to leave them in the past, and fulfill ourselves in the present. But, in my case, as unbelievable as all of this was in the beginning, I must tell you I am a better man for the experience. And if all of this has done anything to make you more comfortable with the bigger picture of life, well, then it was well worth the shock!"

The audience once again stood and applauded. Chris was creating a wonderful bond with the students.

"I have a question, as well, Professor."

"Yes, Mrs. Williams?" We had not only attracted the student body with this experiment, but faculty, also. One of our music instructors was speaking in her lilting musical voice.

"When someone is put under and regressed to passed life, do you contact each life in succession starting with the one previous to this and so on?"

I turned to Meredith. "I would like to pass that question along to our hypnosis expert. Meredith, if you would be so kind?"

"In fact, no, Mrs. Williams. There is no apparent pattern in past life recollection. If I specifically ask for an incarnation I have been working with, that experience will come through. But time being the illusion it is, well . . ." Meredith turned to look at me and stepped away from the mike.

"This gets into the area we struggle with so much in class. You are aware of time as events happening one after the other. Life as we know it progresses in a linear fashion. But that is only an illusion for the benefit of our current lifetime and the lessons we choose to learn. Because we accepted the axiom of time and space in this reality, we operate under those conditions. The term we use, reincarnation, implies a series of lifetimes in a linear fashion, as well. Truthfully, they follow no such rule.

Our current focus is in one incarnation. But the nature of our souls is such that we operate on different levels of awareness simultaneously. It's as though we are broken off from the main source, an oversoul, if you will, and we coexist with our incarnations in a collateral or parallel fashion, like the individual layering of a single onion. So in reality, the term 'past life is' a misnomer. 'Parallel life' might be more accurate. But we use the term 'past life' because it makes sense within the confines of the linear world we exist in. If you are more confused than before you asked, don't worry; time and its illusive nature is a constant enigma to all my classes!" We heard little comments of "That's the truth!" and laughter throughout the audience.

All in all the assembly went well.

# Chapter 13

LISA KELLY AMES - MISSING - ANYONE WITH
INFORMATION, PLEASE CONTACT . . .

This was the type of headline that attracted the Angels. Lisa Kelly Ames lived in Louisiana. Baton Rouge to be exact. She was last seen at her day-care center, under the strict supervision of several child-care workers. Lunch was served, and during the rush of it, somehow Lisa Kelly disappeared.

The Baton Rouge police were called. Frightened beyond reason, Marilyn Cross was on the verge of hysterics. She had thought that after a good search of the building in which her day-care center was housed and the surrounding grounds, Lisa Kelly would be found. In her out of control imagination, far too much time had lapsed between the search and the arrival of the police.

"Description? Yes, you need a description. The child is five years old. Average height and weight for her age. Her hair is shoulder length, light brown. She has very large blue eyes. She was wearing jeans and a lilac sweatshirt that said "Grandma's Darling." Ms. Cross began to shake at the thought of this little girl not going home tonight. "What have we done? How could we just lose her?"

"I'm sure you are doing everything you're supposed to do, Ms. Cross. Don't give up hope. She could turn up at any minute. Most do. Now, tell me about your staff. Are your workers all assembled here?"

"Yes, of course. We've all been looking for her."

At that moment a woman approached Ms. Cross. "I don't think that's correct. We can't find Dorothy, Ms. Cross."

"Dorothy is one of your staff? When did you last see her?"

"She was helping with lunch as she usually does. Maybe she is outside looking for Lisa."

Sergeant Connor shook his head. "No, I'm afraid we told everyone to meet inside and stay together. The rest of my officers are outside. They would have sent her in here by now. I will need a description of Dorothy and any information you can give me starting with how long she's been in your employ."

"Well, Dorothy is a young woman, in her early thirties, 5'7", short blonde hair, and green eyes. She has worked here for five years. Really, Sergeant, this is a waste of time. Dorothy is a very reliable, levelheaded woman. Why just a few months ago her marriage broke up. She lost a child in an accident several years ago. But through it all, she has remained a reliable, exemplary employee. She would do anything for these children, Sergeant. She is devoted to them. Surely she would never abduct one of them!"

"Maybe not, but I will need all of this information just in case. We have to follow any available lead, Ms. Cross, if we are to find the child."

The newspaper article told of a missing child and child-care worker. Dorothy Carlton missing; Lisa Kelly Ames thought to be in her company. The Angels had an advantage the police didn't have: Astral Travel enabling us to think of someone and find ourselves immediately in their presence. As we visualized Lisa and Dorothy, we were suddenly transported in spirit to a poolside apartment complex in Ft. Myers, Florida. We listened to a conversation between Lisa Kelly and Dorothy, her abductor. Lisa Kelly's babyish charm was enhanced by her childish voice and sweet Louisiana drawl.

"I know you want to go home, Lisa. You've told me that often enough. And I have explained that your mom asked me to take you on a vacation while she did some work. She wanted you to have a fun vacation. Aren't you having fun here? I thought you would love Florida."

"Yes, Miss Dorothy, but I would like to be with my Mama. I could help her with her work. I am a big girl, you know! Mama always likes it when I help her clean the house. She says I am a big help!"

"I know, Dear. Now go off and play. You will see your Mama soon enough."

As usual we waited to get the child alone. We watched out of sight as Dorothy prepared and fed Lisa her supper.

It was difficult not to feel sorry for Dorothy. She was obviously distracted by her own grief over losing a child. The loving way she cared for Lisa Kelly made her pain that much more apparent. Finally, she tucked Lisa in after the two of them said their prayers, with a special prayer said by Lisa for her Mama.

The door closed behind Dorothy, and we waited a short time for them to settle in.

"Lisa. Lisa Kelly." Meredith called to the child, waking her out of the sleep she was quickly falling into. She sat straight up in bed.

"Who are you?"

"We're friends of your Mama's. She's finished with her work, and she would like you to come home now. She sent us to find you and bring you back." Meredith approached Lisa alone.

"I can go home? Oh, yes! I miss my Mama!"

"Good! She misses you, too! Get dressed now, and we'll go."

Things were progressing smoothly, until the door opened. Dorothy stood in shock looking straight at us! "Who are you? Who let you into this apartment?"

"Oh my God! She can see us!" Alex's reaction voiced what we were all thinking.

"We have come for the child. She must be returned." I used the most authoritative voice I had to work with.

"That doesn't tell me how you got into this room! Where did you come from?" With that, Dorothy lunged forward grabbing for Meredith's arm. The rest of the Angels approached in a body to intercept her, not realizing how unnecessary that move was. Dorothy's hand passed right through Meredith's arm.

"What are you, some kind of a hologram?"

"I think they're angels, Miss Dorothy! I have been praying to see my Mama and they came! They must be angels!"

Alex spoke up before anyone could stop her. "That's rich! You kidnap this child, and you want to know who we are? You have some nerve, Lady! You ought to be thinking about all the time you will spend in prison for this little stunt!"

Mark was moved by Dorothy's plight and tried to help diffuse Alex's anger. "Alex, have a little compassion. Can't you see this woman is not acting in her right mind?"

Dorothy sat down on the floor sobbing. Seeing this, Lisa Kelly crawled out of bed and sat in Dorothy's lap with her arms around her neck. Meredith took over.

"You know this child must be returned, Dorothy." Meredith's

tone was gentle and understanding. "Your daughter, her name was Lisa, also. Wasn't it? She would have been five years old this year."

"That's right. How did you know that?"

"You are very psychic, Dorothy. You would not be able to see us if you weren't. I know these things for that very same reason. I know you meant Lisa Kelly no harm. You just missed your own little girl. Isn't that right, Dorothy?"

Dorothy clung to Lisa, crying so hard she could only nod her head to respond. She made a valiant effort to control herself and dried her tears. "Everything went with my Lisa. I felt like I should have gone with her, too.

My marriage started failing from that day on. Without her, life just isn't worth living."

"You need some help, Dorothy. You've held these feelings back far too long, and look where it has gotten you. First, the child must be safely returned. Then you must get some professional help."

"You're in spirit, aren't you? You are some kind of angels?"

"I don't know about being angels, but, yes, we are in spirit."

"That means Lisa is alive!"

"Of course she is. Would you like me to teach you to call to her? You can learn to see her as you see us. Bree has had experience in this area. Bree would you join us?"

"Certainly. I'd love to help."

Meredith and Bree moved into the hallway and turned beckoning Dorothy to follow. We stayed with Lisa Kelly while they were gone. When they returned, Dorothy looked like a different person. She seemed much more confident and in control of her emotions. "I will call the police and turn myself in. Will you wait with me?"

The Ft. Myers officers were there within minutes. Two squad

cars arrived simultaneously. Lisa Kelly was allowed to say good-bye to Dorothy, then was kept in another room as they led Dorothy away. The officers were sensitive to Dorothy's plight, reassuring her that she made the right choice. Dorothy was hand-cuffed, a seemingly unnecessary and robotic gesture, and put into a squad car. Lisa Kelly, chattering away about the group of angels who helped Dorothy and herself, happily walked hand in hand with the officer who facilitated the first part of her journey home.

Although Meredith enjoyed keeping a scrapbook of the articles on our success stories, the Angels had long since stopped searching out local newspapers for the information they already had. We knew the child was returned. We did not need to see it in print.

What we hadn't expected was a headline that swept the newspaper industry from one coast to the other. The headline implied that there were guardian angels watching over a little girl in Ft. Myers, Florida. Guardian angels implored a grief-stricken Dorothy Carlton to turn herself in to the police and return Lisa Kelly Ames.

Calls started pouring in from all over the country with stories of mysteriously found children who had all insisted that they were returned to their families with the help of angels. Suddenly, there were newscasts on both television and radio mulling over the accounts of angel assistance for abducted and missing children. A station in Chicago asked for viewer participation in a poll asking whether or not they believed in angel intervention. And Dorothy, from a women's prison awaiting trial, made the talk show circuit! We all watched as Dorothy described her "angels" on national television, specifically the "Emily Taylor Show". I walked into the Counseling Center just as the show was beginning. Alex, Mark, Louis, Amy, Bree, and Meredith sat transfixed in front of the television.

"Professor, look, we are about to have our cover blown on national television!" Mark was highly distressed by this possibility.

"Really? What are you watching?"

"Emily Taylor. She's interviewing Dorothy Carlton from her prison cell in Baton Rouge."

We quietly listened.

"Can you fill us in on the details of the kidnapping, Dorothy?"

"Emily, I don't know what got into me. I had been watching Lisa Kelly since she started attending Sunny Vale Day Care Center. She reminded me so much of my own daughter. My child, whose name was also Lisa, died at age three in a terrible accident. She drowned in a neighbor's pool. They had turned their backs for only a minute! But that's all it took. Lisa Kelly had features similar to my Lisa. We had become friends almost instantly. I played with her more than the other children. I just couldn't help myself. I guess I just lost my mind, I have no other explanation. But I thought that somehow I could keep Lisa Kelly, and she would become my little girl. I convinced myself that her appearance was no coincidence. I thought Lisa Kelly looked like my Lisa because somehow my Lisa was coming back to me."

"And so, after lunch at the Sunny Vale Day Care Center, you simply walked away with her, and took her to an apartment you keep in Ft. Myers, Florida?"

"That's correct, Emily."

"I am certain I express the feelings of the audience, as well as myself, when I tell you that we sympathize with the loss of your own little girl. It must have been a devastating experience. Tell us, please, how you decided to turn yourself in and return Lisa Kelly to her family."

"It was our second night in Ft. Myers. I had given Lisa Kelly her dinner and tucked her in for the night. My room was just across the hall, and I heard a strange woman's voice. At first I thought Lisa Kelly had turned on the television set in her room. I thought that might lull her to sleep, so I didn't do anything about it. But I kept listening and soon realized the woman was speaking specifically to Lisa Kelly. I became afraid and rushed into Lisa Kelly's room. There I saw a woman at Lisa's bedside and behind her were six more people! I panicked and went to grab the woman closest to Lisa. But my hand passed right through her arm!"

"Now, wait a minute. You touched this woman, but your hand passed through her?"

"That's right. Lisa Kelly was convinced they were angels there to take her home to her Mama. I didn't know what to think. One of them in the background became very angry with me. Another told her to have some compassion. And the woman near Lisa's bed told me I had done a terrible thing, but that she understood why. She knew about my daughter and that she would have been five years old this year, as Lisa Kelly is. She knew my daughter's name was also Lisa. I asked how she knew these things and she told me she was psychic just as I was. I never knew I was psychic, but I must be if I can see angels!"

"Dorothy, just how do you know these people were angels?"

"Well, like I said, I couldn't touch them, my hand passed right through. And the woman who was speaking to me told me I could use my ability to see my real daughter again. She and another angel took me to another room. We sat and closed our eyes. She told me to call to my Lisa, and when I opened my eyes she was in front of me!"

"You saw your daughter who had drowned?"

"That's right. But she's older. She looked to be about five. The age she would be if she were alive today."

"Did your daughter say anything to you, Dorothy?"

"Yes, she said, 'I am here with you, Mommy. I can visit whenever you call.'" Dorothy needed some time to recover from this recollection. A hand reached in from off camera and offered her a tissue.

"I realize this is an emotional issue for you, Dorothy."

"I'm all right."

"The fact that you returned the child will weigh in your favor during your trial. But you do realize you are facing a serious charge?"

"It doesn't matter. I know my little girl is still alive. She's being cared for and she's not suffering. That's all that is important to me. She has people who care for her and love her. And one day, we will be together again. Nothing in this world could make me unhappy now because I know someday I will be with my Lisa again. That is the gift the angels gave me."

Emily, with tears in her eyes, thanked her guest and the connection was dropped.

Returning her attention to her audience, she said, "We might assume that Dorothy's story of intervening angels is one she made up for an insanity defense. At least that is what many of the newspapers are implying. I don't know about you, but I felt quite a lot of sincerity in her interview. And we can't dismiss the accounts of angels helping children in crisis all over this country. Can Dorothy and all of these children be suffering from the same kind of hysteria? I would like to think not. I would like to think that there are angels out there watching over each and every one of us, especially the children."

So Emily Taylor's show was ended on a note of hope.

"What do we do now?" Alex submitted this question to no one in particular, in an obvious state of agitation.

"Do, Alex? What do we do about what?"

"Professor, Emily Taylor just announced to the world that

angels are returning lost children! Our secret is out in the open! How can we continue our work?"

"I think you're getting worked up over nothing, Alex. This is all speculation; no secret has been revealed. I think it was a great story. Emily handled the interview with sensitivity and there was no harm done."

"No harm done? Every psychic in the world is going to be looking for us!"

"Good! Then maybe they will join our cause and help all the children who are suffering. Even the ones who are not lost or stolen. We could use all the help we can get!"

"But, Professor!"

"But nothing, Alex. The professor is right." Louis's tone showed his impatience. "Trust me, they won't catch on. After all, Alex, you're no angel!"

"Now, now, let's not take shots here, Louis. None of us is an angel. So we got a little publicity. I don't think it will hurt. Chances are it will go by way of all headlines, forgotten in a week. And if not, so be it. We couldn't have a better cover than the angels phenomenon. After all, angel intervention is thought of as a gift. It's not as though they could hunt us down and put us under a microscope. We couldn't have better protection. No, our work will go on as planned. And if we make more headlines, that will be fine with me. As long as they're headlines with happy endings."

# Chapter 14

Carrie Wattson and her twin brother Matt were born cocaine addicted. Their quiet fight for life in separate incubators, aided by tubes and machines, was a pathetic sight. But that was nothing compared to the horrors these innocent children would have to endure just to have a chance in this world. They were African-American children born to a mother speeding through life on cocaine; she never saw her children after they were taken from her. As they grew stronger and started to gain weight, they went to a home for children born to addiction. The woman who ran this institution, Janine Jefferson, herself an African American, had great sympathy for the plight of these children. With little federal aid and few donations, she struggled to keep the door open so that these babies would have some sort of home in their infancy. The local government assisted, as well, finding foster care for some of the children when so many in need of help threatened to overcome Janine's efforts.

Janine could never turn away a child. She would just have to make do. And that was the beginning for Carrie and Matt. Janine called them her "sweet babies." She was happy when a state social worker informed her that a two-parent household ready to take these children had been found. She was happy because she knew these parents could give the children a decent start in life; but it was so hard to say good-bye.

From all outward appearances, the home of Joseph and Phyllis Iverson seemed to be an answered prayer. Phyllis, a highly regarded mathematician, took time from her career and chose to stay at home and care for the babies. Joseph, also an educator, was an extremely gifted man with a genius intelligence. All outward appearances indicated a stable, protected environment. But as we have all come to realize, outward appearances can be deceiving.

Mrs. Iverson hid a problem that was about to rage out of control. A problem of which even she was unaware. A victim of child abuse, the horrors of which were buried deep in her subconscious, Phyllis had survived by creating a variety of personalities. Most were harmless and went unnoticed. Her husband explained them as products of a theatrical imagination and he was often amused by her "role playing": a young child at play, a mother interested in the infants' welfare, a teacher interested in the further education of school-age children. Although the different personalities took turns, they were enough alike that no one seemed to guess there was a problem. But with the homecoming of the infant twins, the first babies to enter Phyllis's life, another personality began to emerge.

This one was not harmless. It demonstrated the monstrous abuse Phyllis Iverson was subjected to as a child. Having the twin infants in her home helped to bring this evil personality to the surface. Joseph Iverson never saw the abuse. How could he know?

The babies were too small to complain, and Phyllis did not bother him with the everyday duties of bathing, changing, etc. So the cigarette burns, cuts, and bruises went unnoticed.

In fact, Phyllis had no recollection of where they came from. By the time she had calmed down long enough to care for the children, the oppressive, evil personality had submerged to its depths, leaving a kind, motherly woman in its place. No one knew. But that was not completely true. Unaware of why she was dreaming such nightmares, Clarissa Wattson would dream of the babies she gave up. At first she would see them and awaken in tears. But the dreams were recurring and progressive, until she saw the signs of abuse on their little bodies in clear detail. Then, finally, Clarissa dreamed of Phyllis, the perpetrator harming these innocent children. Drugged or not, instinct took over and Clarissa was determined to find her babies. She started with the hospital where she had given birth. The staff was not helpful. They were not about to help a drug addict find her children after she had abandoned them. They accused Clarissa of abusing drugs to the point that her nightmares were out of control. But Clarissa knew better. She would find her babies and she would not leave that hospital until she knew where they had been taken.

A loud argument ensued, and the hospital administrator interceded. The duty nurse apologized for the noise and explained to Mr. Winfield that Clarissa was causing a scene and would not leave. She was about to call security. Mr. Winfield was a kind man, and something about the desperate young woman tugged at his heart. He thought he might calm her down and send her on her way if he listened to her story. So the two of them went to the lounge to talk. Mr. Winfield listened as Clarissa described her nightmares. Something about Clarissa made him think that they were not nightmares brought on by drugs. Noting that Clarissa was obviously sober, he was caught up in the possibility of a horrible nightmare coming true. But on the other hand, he believed she might have been dealing with the horror of her own guilt. Whatever the reason for the nightmares, Mr. Winfield saw no harm in allowing Clarissa to talk to the woman who nurtured her children for the first few months of their lives.

"Many of the babies born addicted are sent to Janine Jefferson. From there, the state finds foster homes for them. I will give you Ms. Jefferson's address. I am sure she would be happy to talk to you. She is a very kind woman, Clarissa. She will no doubt put your mind at ease." From the hospital, Clarissa Wattson took a bus deeper into Cleveland's inner city. Janine Jefferson welcomed Clarissa at the door. After hearing about her terrible nightmares, she attempted to reassure her.

"Of course, I remember your babies, Ms. Wattson. They were the sweetest things. But you mustn't worry. They went to a fine family for foster care. Two teachers who live in Claret, Ohio. It's a wealthy suburb. I am positive they are all right. I met them myself and I can tell you, you have nothing to worry about."

Janine Jefferson was a sincere and kind woman, just as Mr. Winfield had described her. Clarissa believed her. Relieved and certain she would have no further nightmares, Clarissa thanked Janine and left. But the nightmares didn't stop. Clarissa returned to Janine three days later.

"Clarissa, I would like to help you, but the state won't allow me to give you information on where they placed the twins. Besides, I know this is all in your mind. Your babies are fine. You have to believe me."

The Angels projected to the home of Mr. and Mrs. Joseph Iverson in Claret. We had no idea why we were there. There was no child we were looking for, but each of us had projected at the same time during group meditation and found ourselves surrounding a double crib. The children were fully clothed, and we did not see the evidence of their abuse. But we didn't have to. Their auras were flickering like tiny flames desperately trying to get a breath of air. Insights flashed through our minds playing information, as if in movie form, of the children's desperate situation.

Louis asked, "How is this happening? It's like a bad movie going through my head! Am I the only one experiencing this?"

"No, Louis, I see it, too," Amy responded immediately.

Each in turn acknowledged seeing the terrible bodily inflictions these children were subjected to.

"Where is this coming from?" Alex half screamed the question, responding to the terrifying scenes being played in her head.

"From the infants," Meredith's response was to the point. "They are communicating to us in spirit."

"How can they do that?"

"They are babies, Mark. Would you like to live in such a tiny shell?"

That was too brief an explanation from me and Meredith continued, "Some people call them guardian angels because the spirit of an infant will walk beside the child until they are comfortable with remaining in the body for longer periods of time. Those who are psychic enough to witness this phenomena automatically assume the child has a personal angel. But it is their own spirits which cannot operate comfortably in such a tiny body, and worse, through an undeveloped brain.

"Well, if there are two spirits here with us, why can't we see them?"

"Because, Alex, they are not completely here. These babies may not survive and their spirits are waiting in another space. That's the reason for the weak auras around their bodies."

"So they are being abused by someone in this house? By their mother?"

"I don't think so, Louis. I don't sense the presence of their mother. I believe it's a stranger. But it is a woman, a caregiver." As Meredith spoke, I sensed a penetrating evil in this room.

"So what do we do? We can't just pick them up and carry them off! Even if we could, where would we take them?"

"All good questions, Alex. First, let's say some quiet prayers around these cribs. If we can, we must send healing energy to these babies. They are ready to leave these bodies permanently."

"Do you mean they could die, Professor?"

"Yes, Amy. It is their choice. But if they believe we can help them, they may wait a bit longer."

We joined hands and silently sent energy and prayers to two babies lying quietly side by side in their cribs. Their auras seemed to soak up the energy, giving them a bit of color and more consistency.

"We will be back, Little Ones." Meredith never broke a promise.

Reluctantly we returned to the counseling center and our sleeping bodies.

"So now what, Professor?" Alex tried vainly to hide her feelings.

"We are going to listen to what Meredith is planning." I could tell by the look on her face that she was on top of this dilemma.

"We need help, physical, three-dimensional intervention. Just before we returned, I made a point of seeing the name of the town we were in. It's a suburban section of Cleveland, Ohio, called Claret. Someone comes to mind in that area, a man who has brought much attention to himself through his work. He is an advanced spirit and he is also a doctor of psychiatry. He works with people in past life therapy."

"A physician working with reincarnation?" Louis reiterated in partial disbelief.

"That's right, Louis. He regresses patients to find reasons for their various problems and at some point in his career, he discovered a patient's past life. He is very open about it, much to the dismay of his peers. But he is a spiritually powerful man, and has had so much success with past life resolution that he ignores his fellow psychiatrists and does what he was trained to do, help his patients. I have met this gentleman briefly; and tonight, we will all meet him."

It was pre-dawn as we all sat comfortably in our chairs and thought of Dr. Ryan Murphy. Within moments, we were in a room watching him sleep. As I had done many times before, we summoned the spirit of Dr. Murphy from his body.

"Please forgive the intrusion, Doctor, but we need your help."

"Who are you people?" Looking directly at Meredith, he said, "Do I know you?"

"Yes, Doctor. We met briefly at a lecture on reincarnation. During a break you confided in me about your work in past life regression. I am Meredith Tolworth."

"The psychic, of course! I remember now." He looked from Meredith to the rest of us, and as he was turning, he noticed his body which remained sleeping in his bed. "Oh my God! Am I dead?"

"No. You're all right, Dr. Murphy. You simply have astral projected. You are in no danger." Meredith's soothing voice reassured this astonished man. "We would not have come this dramatically, but our need is great. The lives of two infants are at stake, Doctor."

That got his attention. "Two infants? Who? Where?"

"Take my hand." Once again we all stood surrounding two cribs and two small babies. "If you notice, Doctor, their auras are flickering. We must work quickly. We could lose them."

Dr. Murphy, addressing Meredith, expressed his confusion. "How can I help? What's wrong with them?"

"They are being physically abused by a woman with multiple

personalities. She's a foster parent and is unaware of her own behavior. But, somehow, we must get them away from her. They will not survive if we don't."

"How? What am I to do? Where are we?" In his confusion, Dr. Murphy asked questions without waiting for answers.

"We are in the home of Phyllis and Joseph Iverson."

"The Iversons? I know these people. That's impossible! They are well established educators."

Dr. Murphy was familiar enough with the Iversons not to take our accusations as a matter of fact. He needed convincing.

"Mrs. Iverson is a well-established educator with a dark past, and secrets even she is unaware of, Dr. Murphy. They are secrets so horrible she is incapable of remembering. She needs your intervention, Doctor. These children need your intervention if they are to survive." Dr. Murphy listened intently as I pointed out that there was no time to explain the phenomena he was experiencing. He had precious little time left to act and he was our only hope.

Those words reverberated in Dr. Murphy's head as he woke from what he believed to be a strange nightmare. His daily routine took on subliminal qualities, and the subject of his dream seemed to be his only reality. Unable to shake the disturbing thoughts, he drove to the Iverson residence. Phyllis answered the door.

"Dr. Murphy! Ryan! We haven't seen you in ages! How have you been?"

"Never mind that, Phyllis. I want to see your foster children. I want to see them now!"

Unaware of any problem, Phyllis was stunned by Dr. Murphy's brusque, unkind display. "Well, of course, Ryan. They're upstairs."

Shoving her aside, he ran up the stairs with Phyllis close at his heels. Recognizing the house, the hallway, and finally the infants' nursery from the dream, he found it quickly and with no hesitation. "Remove their gowns, Phyllis."

"What?"

"I said remove their gowns. Do it now!" Dr. Murphy's agitation was increasing and fear began to grip Phyllis Iverson. She did what she was told.

The bruised, burned, pathetic little bodies seemed to shock Phyllis, as she stepped back in apparent disbelief. "How could this have happened?"

"You did this, Phyllis."

"Me? Certainly not! I could never . . . !"

Dr. Murphy grabbed both her arms and sat her in a chair. Yelling at the top of his lungs and reducing Phyllis to an hysterical shaking mass, he said, "You did this!" Seeing her obvious fear and confusion, he then softened his approach. "You have serious problems, Phyllis. You have to concentrate on getting the help you need. But first we must get these children away from you to safety." He phoned the hospital and requested an ambulance.

But the Angels' work was not done. After leaving Dr. Murphy to his dream, we went straight to Clarissa. The dream she experienced caused her to understand just how much she loved her babies. Between pictures of her tormented children she heard the voices of the "Angels". "Save your babies, Clarissa. They need their mother. They need you." She tossed and turned for the rest of the night until she awoke, dressed and, without knowing why, headed for the hospital.

Dr. Murphy, the twins and Clarissa all arrived at the same time. Clarissa, seeing her twins taken from the ambulance, ran to their side. Dr. Murphy intercepted her. "You are their mother, aren't you?"

"Yes, I'm Clarissa Wattson. What happened to them?"

"They will be all right. They need to stay here for a couple of days. Are you ready to take back your responsibility?"

Tears flooded Clarissa's face as her children were strapped on a stretcher and wheeled into the emergency room. "I thought they would be cared for!"

"They need you, Clarissa. If you will work very hard, I will help you. Your babies need their mother. They need you."

# Chapter 15

L ife seems to spin in its endless pursuit to catch up with
itself. Of course it never does! But as we watch it unfold,
to our amazement, the days pass in rapid succession.

Once again, Calvert bloomed forth a splendid summertime.
Regaled in nature's finest, our lovely town came alive with color
and scent. With the dawning of summer life came a project in
which all of us had some involvement: Bree's wedding. Because
of the sensitivity of this description, I feel I would not do it justice.
I turn you over to Meredith's capable and detailed recollection.

Chris had finally asked her. He took Bree to his uncle's home
in Downer Woods. Memories flooded back as she entered the
grand Victorian, met the rest of Chris's relatives, and enjoyed their
company for the evening. Later she would explain to me that she
had felt so at home. Of course, Chris understood these feelings,
but the rest of the Tait family would have to remain uninformed.
After dinner, Chris took Bree for a walk in the English garden

behind the house. Under a well-lit moon, he slipped her engagement ring on her finger, and asked if he might try again! Surely, I do not have to tell you Bree's response!

The wedding was planned with little extra time for all the lavish arrangements. It would be in July, in the grand ballroom of Bree's family home. When the day finally came, white roses and a variety of orchids graced the ballroom. Seating was arranged on either side of an aisle, and the couple married under an extravagantly sculptured canopy laced with satin ribbon and doting flowers.

It seemed the entire town had been looking for an invitation to this occasion. But the guest list had to be limited to a cozy two hundred people.

Bree had asked Lang and me to give her away. In order to facilitate this request, it was necessary to rewrite tradition. I stood near the minister, holding Bree's wedding bouquet and watched as Lang walked her down the aisle. She wore a detailed Victorian wedding gown Beth was never able to wear. Traditional white satin and lace, tightly drawn to her waist, then flowing down the aisle. Exquisite tiny satin tea roses, enhanced with pearls, decorated the gown from the bodice to the tip of the extensive train. In her hands was a small bouquet of roses, which she offered to Chris's mother just as she approached the canopied attendants. Then she turned to me. I kissed her cheek and offered her the magnificent bridal bouquet, a stunning arrangement of tightly assembled fragrant white roses just as Beth's bouquet of the nineteenth century would have been designed. Fighting the tears trying to escape, I glanced passed the lovely bride. I could not help my attention being drawn to Lang, frustratingly trying to gesture with some discretion in the background.

What in heaven's name was he trying to tell me? He looked over dramatically to his right, and, following his gaze, I saw them: two faint images standing hand in hand. These two were not of this world. The Lambeau's apparently were not about to miss their daughter's wedding. I smiled and nodded first to them, and then to Lang in recognition of our special guests. The scene touched me deeply. I stood spellbound watching them as they listened to the minister's words and gazed upon their beautiful daughter. When the ceremony was finished, they looked over at me. I smiled and they returned the smile. As Gabrielle and Christopher turned to walk down the aisle as husband and wife, they stepped one on either side. Bree's mother slipped her hand in her daughter's and her father put his arm around his new son-in-law. Then they disappeared.

I couldn't help but ponder the concept of a wonderful world where we all could sense the nurturing love surrounding us from other dimensions. It is a gift we would all come to welcome, if we only could learn to see beyond what our physical eyes perceive.

Photographs were taken in the garden, with the guests mingling among tables laden with finely prepared h'ors d'oeuvres, cordials, and splits of champagne. The ballroom was being set for a feast, with the orchestra tuning up in the background.

At the end of the meal, tables were cleared away, seating was arranged around the dance floor, and the orchestra leader called for the first dance of the bride and groom. Some Debussy piece played sweetly by this group of fine musicians, you expect? No. An antique gramophone was carefully lifted to a place of honor under a spotlight. It dutifully played an old recording, scratches and all, of a Victorian piece. And so the couple danced their first dance as husband and wife to a melody from the year 1901 called "Trust Me With Your Heart Again."

The couple's haunting love story had made them somewhat famous. All of the guests knew the significance of the Victorian decor, and all the lovely Victorian touches that made this wedding a fairy tale with a long- awaited happy ending.

Love, traveling through time, to reunite lovers. True love never dies, even though we may part company for a time. It is only the illusion of time before we are united again. The young couple looked exquisite together and we all knew we would rarely, if ever, see them apart again. They left on their honeymoon cruise and have been joyously happy ever since. Lang and I try not to interfere too much, but we so enjoy being in their company. Their happiness is contagious and their home, the Lambeaus' grand Victorian, has become a peaceful sanctuary.

Thank you, Meredith, for the woman's touch.

# Chapter 16

The publicity on angel intervention seemed to be dying down. As I expected, it made little or no difference in our continuing work.

Chris was let in on our secret, since he had experienced and learned so much. He became a fan of meditation, the results of which fascinated him to the extent that he couldn't keep himself from recommending it to nearly everyone he spoke to. Because of his advancing awareness, Bree thought he should understand about the work that was so important to her. She wanted no secrets in her marriage, and she wanted him to be able to share the happiness she felt guiding a child back to its family.

Chris did not become a participant in our mission to return lost children. Astral projection seemed too other worldly for him to experiment with. After expressing concern over his wife's safety, Meredith offered him the log she kept on all our missing children. He was quite impressed with the number of children whose lives we had impacted. He was especially impressed with the follow-up articles and clippings that graced nearly every newspaper in the country. He surmised that Bree was in no danger, was obviously gifted and fortunate to be a part of this group, and wished us all continued success.

Children were returned home by whatever clever means we could come up with during our spiritual travels. We knew the gratitude and happiness of their parents. We felt some of those joyous feelings ourselves.

Many of our excursions were precipitated by articles we read in newspapers, flyers sent out through the mail, photographs printed on milk cartons, etc. Occasionally we would simply project and allow fate to lead us where it may, somehow sensing an urgency for which there was no physical request.

All of these children became precious to us and the energy flow between us was stimulating and encouraged us to continue our work. It was also beneficial in teaching us of the infinite forms in which energy abides. As testimony to the old saying, "I thought I had seen it all!", we are still learning astounding secrets from our own universe.

On a clear crisp evening, the Angels assembled at the counseling center for a meditation, dinner, and conversation.

We sat in our drawing room, fire lit. October's chill hinted of winter's approach. But we were comfortable and in good company. Meredith hadn't spoken much that evening, and knowing her as well as I do, I was aware something important was on her mind.

"Are you going to let us in on it, Meredith?" I had turned to my right where she was seated next to me.

"Excuse me?"

"You've been anywhere but here this evening. What's troubling you?"

"Nothing really, Lang. I can't help but feel we have to be somewhere soon. Somewhere other than here that we can't go to physically."

"Well, we can project if you think we should, Meredith." Louis saw the work of the Angels as his life's work. He believed that regardless of the path life may lead him on, nothing he could do would ever be as important or life affirming as being one of the Angels. Because of this, he never felt put out, or invaded in any way when it came to his work as an Angel. To Louis, as I expect the rest of us, this was a gift to be practiced above all else.

"Good, Louis. I think we should." Meredith quickly agreed.

It had become a simple process of relaxation, deep breathing, and envisioning our surroundings. It was a sensation of forcing energy upward and then, magically, released, not at all a frightening experience, rather invigorating, if a description were needed.

In the astral state, recognizing each other, we formed a circle and let our mission overcome us.

Our next awareness was in a damp dark cabin engulfed in thick green woods. Where we were was not readily apparent, but a feeling of intense depression was shared among us.

A child acknowledged us immediately, surprisingly so, due to her age. This young girl, at the point of becoming a young woman, was able to sense our presence completely. Quickly we surmised other unusual facts, the answers to which would become clear with time. The child's dress was not of this decade. This could have many explanations: a child who came from a family with little funds, wearing dresses made to fit from her grandmother's closet, or abducted in the middle of a dress rehearsal for a school play! But the fact that she was at least twelve years old and yet aware of the presence of the projected spirits that stood before her alerted me to the fact that this was no ordinary lost child.

Mimma was a dear thing. Her face glowed with delight in seeing us, instinctively knowing she had been saved. Innocently, she came toward us and tears of joy began to flow.

"Can you help me? I am Mimma. I am so lost!" Mimma needn't have asked. Her plea was unnecessary. Certainly that was the reason we were there. "My uncle brought me here in his wagon. We were to go into town to do Mother's errands, but he never took me to town. He took me here. And I didn't know him after that. He became so cruel; he started to drink and he hit me when I told him I wanted to go . . ."

Questions whirled in my head. Wagon? Did she mean horse drawn wagon? Why would they go to town in a wagon? Maybe this man collected such memorabilia, but why use such a conspicuous vehicle to abduct a child? Or could we have inadvertently ended up in a different time period? Had we projected to the past? Alex looked over at me with the same look of confusion on her face as the rest of us. I shook my head and shrugged my shoulders.

"Mimma, where do you belong? Where is your family?" Meredith's voice had lost its maternal comforting tones and showed more concern than usual. It was obvious there were questions for which we had no answers. In addition, Meredith and I sensed swirling, menacing energy around us. The rest were thankfully oblivious to this presence, or they might have returned, posthaste, to their bodies. We saw no point in alerting them, and communicated only to each other of our simultaneous knowing. It was a disturbing presence, dangerous and consuming. With all of our experience, we felt equally uneasy and somehow threatened.

"Mother lives with Grandfather on the farm west of Rolling Hills."

"In what state, Mimma?"

"What state? This one, of course! Kentucky!"

"Do you know how long the ride was from your home to this cabin, or better, to the nearest town?" I was trying to get some bearings and hoped the girl had enough sense of direction to help locate her home, if in fact we were in Kentucky. This was an assumption I was beginning to doubt.

"It was about an hour, but he left after the last time he . . ."

"After the last time he what, Mimma?"

"After he beat me. He's not been back for days. I must go home! It's so frightening here!" Mimma broke down in tears, not understanding how anyone, especially her uncle, could be so cruel to her.

As for her fear, I sympathized with those feelings. Somehow, she was not alone, but the energy that filled this room was not of a benevolent nature. Mimma sat in a chair turning her face from us. Fresh blood stained her otherwise flaxen colored hair. The child had been hit severely. A blow to the head which caused a terrible bleeding. It was incredible that she would be conscious, let alone moving about, after such a vicious attack.

"He hasn't been back, so why haven't you left this place?" Louis's inquiry forced Mimma to dry her tears and ponder the question.

"I can't. I've tried, but I always end up back here." A pitiful look of desperation distorted her young face. Alex thought she meant that she was lost, would walk in a circle in the woods, and end up where she started. It was a feasible explanation, but I was beginning to form my own thoughts as to what the problem really was. I looked over at Meredith who, after reading my expression, said, "It might be a good idea to try once more. We will go with you, Mimma."

The child went to the bed and picked up a wrap. Covering her shoulders, she looked like a figure from the past, her skirt falling nearly to her ankles, made of a durable but plain cotton fabric. The shawl that she held so tightly to her looked handmade. The front door to the cabin was open. Nothing held this child prisoner, and no other human was in sight. We walked her to the door and stepped outside. Mimma disappeared.

"Where did she go? She was right in front of me!" Louis was shocked to have lost sight of her. All six of us looked about as if she had hidden right there among us. But, of course, she hadn't. I turned to look inside the cabin. "She's back inside, Louis."

"Well, I didn't see her walk back!"

"I know; something is not right."

Meredith had already returned to the child's side. "Shall we try again, Mimma?"

"Yes, please. I want to go home and see my mother." Her tearful pleas made us want to try to help her all the more. But I knew it would not work, and it didn't.

At her second return, she wept uncontrollably. "I will be stuck in here forever!"

"No, Mimma. No you won't. We will help you somehow." Amy sat near the girl trying in vain to comfort her.

I made a motion to gather the Angels around me. When we thought we were out of Mimma's range of hearing, I said, "Meredith, I think . . ."

"I know, Lang. How do we tell her?"

The rest became impatient and Alex was the first to voice this impatience. "Know! Know what? What in the world is going on here?"

"She's dead, Alex." I put that rather bluntly, but there seemed little I could do to soften the grim reality.

"Dead? She's no more dead than we are!"

"That's an interesting point, Alex, but from a totally physical perspective, I'm afraid Lang is right. Mimma is a spirit with no physical body to return to. The blood in her hair looks as fresh as if she were wounded minutes ago, but her dress is in the style of the mid 1800s, the child of settlers. I think this child has been dead for well over one hundred years, but she's unaware of it."

"Or she doesn't want to be aware of it, Meredith."

"That's probably a more accurate assessment, Bree."

"Well, we can't just leave her like this!" Amy, having returned to the group, wrung her hands.

"No, we will help her, Amy, but we have to do this carefully. We have to be very sensitive to her plight. After all Mimma does not understand her predicament. We have to explain to her that she does not belong in the world she is trying to return to."

"You mean she doesn't belong here." Amy's expression was puzzled.

"No, Amy. We are guests in her reality at the moment. She's not on a physical plane any longer. And the longer she is in this place, the worse things will get. It would not surprise me to hear that she has experienced frightening images and dreams."

"Well, if we are not on the earth plane, then where are we?" Louis's tone was demanding and rising in level to match his excitement and growing fear.

"We're in a place where spirit goes when it has no concept of death." They all turned their attention toward me for a lesson they needed in order to help little Mimma. "This place is a place of lost souls."

"You mean like Purgatory?"

"Sort of, Alex. When a person who believes death is oblivion passes on, he becomes a confused spirit finding that he can still see, feel, and hear. Then he tries to return to his body or his life. That being impossible, he thinks about what it means to be dead and without understanding his powers of creation, creates an environment that reflects that understanding. Of course, it's laden with the typical funerary conceptions he had in life: a coffin, rotting flesh, tormenting thoughts of what happens to the physical body after it breathes its last. It doesn't take long in such an horrific environment to lose one's sanity. The misery found in a place such as I have described is beyond comprehension."

"But we don't see any other spirits here."

"I know you don't, Amy. Be grateful that you don't. But you may have noticed what looked like shiny black marbles floating in and out of that mirror? It's negative energy. If you become more accustomed to this place, you will see more than that. With any luck, we'll be out of here before that happens. Hopefully, any contact Mimma has had with them has been what she interprets as bad dreams. But I assure you, they are here.

Mimma still thinks she's alive, and that has protected her to a limited extent in this environment. A teacher taught me all about the souls that hover over this place, waiting for a glimmer of light over the lost ones. Just asking for help will bring them someone who will raise them from this place. It is crucial we get Mimma the help she needs before she begins to live this nightmare of insanity."

The Angels returned to Mimma's side.

"Why can't I leave this place?"

"You can, Mimma, but not in the way you came. Tell me how you received this terrible cut on your head."

"My uncle. I woke up in this place and he hit me with something very hard. I was asleep afterward, and when I woke up again he was gone."

"Mimma," Meredith slipped her arm around the child. "You may not be able to go to the home you are thinking about."

"What?"

"I am afraid, when you were hit, well, you are not physical anymore."

And the child cried. "I want my mother! I must go home!"

"You will go home, Mimma. Your true home. You have a wonderful place waiting for you. And the people who love you and want to protect you, they are waiting for you also." Meredith's agitation mounted as she tried to overcome the girl's pathetic tears. She was also distressed by the energy forming around us.

Now that Mimma knew she was dead, she had to be carefully guided out of this terrible place, and soon. "You can see your mother again, Mimma. But you have been looking in the wrong place. Your mother is no longer at home, not the home you remember. She is waiting for you in the place she has gone on to."

As Meredith spoke, a cloud or mist seemed to be forming in the corner of the room. It had a soft opalescent glow that descended upon and comforted all of us. Seeing this, Meredith knew she was getting through to the child. Mimma would be all right now. "You need to focus in a different direction. You see, when your uncle hit you, you were unable to survive the blow."

"I am dead!" Mimma's tears were heart wrenching.

"It's not as bad as all that, Mimma. You left your body behind, that's all. But you have been stuck here because you could not imagine there was anything else but your family and farm in Kentucky. There is more, Mimma. The place where your mother and grandfather have gone to, they wait for you there."

The mist was taking shape. Apparently, as we spoke to the child and told her of her new existence, she began to accept her reality. As she did that, the mist gained strength, then form, then solidity and presence. Soon it was in the form of a woman who stood behind Mimma. She stood with her arms outstretched.

"You will have a home there, as well, Mimma. It is a wonderful place. You just have to understand that your world is not the one you remember. You have gone on to a better, gentler place. A place where you will only experience love, and no one will hurt you ever again. You could have seen your mother at any time, but you were focused on going to your house in Kentucky. Your mother has been trying to reach you, probably for a long time now. But you didn't realize she was, and because of that you were unable to see her. You will see her now, Mimma. Your mother has come for you. She will take you home. Turn and greet your mother." Meredith offered a reassuring smile, knowing this terrible journey was about to have a happy ending.

Staring intently at Meredith, Mimma cautiously turned first one shoulder, then her head, until her gaze rested on the woman she had missed for such a terribly long, long time. "Oh! Mother! Oh, Mother, please, please let me come home!" As her mother's arms closed around the child, they stood briefly reuniting in an embrace. Then they seemed to melt from the space we were in.

Mimma was the topic for discussion after our next group meditation.

"How could she be stuck there like that? And for that long? It seems so cruel." Louis questioned Mimma's lengthy difficult experience.

"She really had no concept of how long she was there, Louis. Nor had she any idea that she had left her body and transfixed herself in a place where she became a prisoner. It was her need to get back to her old life that prevented her from moving on to a new one. Just as we saw in the Jameson residence, focus and belief is everything, especially in the spiritual realm, where the creative energy that is thought will control our environment instantly."

"But her mother tried to reach her. Why couldn't she do that, Professor?"

"Again, Amy, it was Mimma's focus that kept her from seeing anything not pertaining to the life she left so abruptly. Her mother was in the world of spirit, and Mimma wanted desperately to remain to finish her physical life. Her choice, her focus, was here. Once she was made to realize how long she had been trapped in this unholy place, and then relinquished her attachment to her former life, she was finally able to move on."

Mimma was all we talked about for months after this experience. Her gentle spirit was kept alive in our hearts through prayers during meditation and through discussions of how she might be progressing. This child, somehow more than the rest, had made a lasting impression on the Angels. We could not forget her. But we knew, after her desperation, she had finally found peace and happiness in a new world.

Our work continued. Karen Slade was a valuable six-year-old, as any would be. But this one had a special talent. The child had the musical ability of a Mozart at the same age as the genius Wolfgang. Her skill at the piano was incredible and she also possessed the creative genius that enabled the master composer to write his first opera at age five. It was not unusual for this child to be away from home for weeks at a time. As her parents readily accepted her fate, she was often on tour with a private tutor, a nanny and a zealous agent. Her agent, Tom Grayhall, from New York, recognized the child's ability after being contacted by the music teacher at her grade school in California, and convinced her parents that this genius belonged to the world of music.

Her life would always be that of a musician, and even at her tender age, he was ready to establish her genius and secure her future. The Slade's wanted nothing but the best for their daughter, and her musical genius needed expressing. They were grateful for Tom Grayhall's interest and his vast knowledge of the world of classical music.

Despite the fact that neither of her parents had any previous experience with music, Karen took to the piano with gusto at age four. Her ability stunned a local piano teacher who consulted the department head of Juilliard. The child was beyond talented. Her mastery and musical sense was inborn, a gift she naturally possessed.

Listening to the child play was a miracle in action. Her love of music, her ability to perform and create belied her years. Margaret and Peter Slade were intelligent in their own right. Their computer expertise enabled them to meet each other while pursuing a degree in computer science, and subsequently carve a life of wealth between them. Margaret, a programmer, and Peter, a systems analyst, were constantly in demand in a world of growing computer fascination. They understood success and the need to make all they could of their talents. Certainly their daughter's talent, totally foreign to them, was none-the-less important.

Unfortunately, Karen's childhood was sacrificed and severely shortened in favor of her musical genius. The child was a national treasure. No classical music enthusiast in this country or the continent of Europe was unfamiliar with her name. Her following and admiration grew daily. Recordings of her piano solos sold at a phenomenal rate. The symphonies she produced were played by every orchestra across both continents. The child was a genius and she was in danger. Karen was in New York on a tour. The previous week's newspaper in New York told of how well Karen was received in concert. Her audience was especially taken with the child's musical expertise when she performed in person, her vast ability contrasted by her unassuming, guileless childish innocence.

Karen's parents were on a jet on their way to New York to help celebrate her sixth birthday. They had plans to spend as much of their vacation as they could in Karen's company. It would be a family vacation and birthday celebration in one trip. Karen's nanny found her missing after the Slades had already boarded the jet for their red-eye flight, so they were not aware of Karen's abduction. Our awareness came in a rather odd fashion the day before it was to occur.

Meredith, among her many gifts, dabbled at the piano. She was quite good, actually, and used her ability as a meditative outlet and hobby. She loved Mozart, and Karen Slade's Mozart-like talent attracted her attention.

It was not unusual for Meredith to pick up Karen's latest CD. She often commented on how greatly she admired Karen Slade's genius. During a session with a client, Karen's music played softly in the background. Meredith listened as her client told of a less-than-happy childhood and the ravaged adult life that followed. But she was unusually drawn to the music, which had been meant only as soothing background accompaniment. A sudden feeling of panic descended over Meredith, and her client stopped in mid-sentence.

"Ms. Tolworth, are you all right?"

"Yes, uh, no. Grace, would you mind if we continued this tomorrow? Something has come up."

"Certainly. I'll reschedule with your secretary."

"Thank you, Dear."

It was three in the afternoon and I was in the middle of my last class of the day. The messenger bolted through the door, obviously inspired by whomever prompted him to get a message to me. I stopped the lecture I was giving and extended my hand to reach for the note. It read, "Assemble the Angels. Hurry. Meredith."

"This is a personal problem that needs immediate attention. I am afraid I will have to cut class short today. We will begin tomorrow where we left off."

As the students filed out of class, I reached for the phone. Finding the Angels took some time. Their classes with me were in the morning. I needed to consult the office for each schedule. I could sense Meredith's agitation, but I was working as quickly as I could. It took less than an hour, but the stress felt like an eternity's worth.

"Meredith? What's wrong?" As we entered the counseling center, we found Meredith pacing the room. She had the cover of Karen Slade's CD in her hands.

"She's in danger. She's about to be abducted. Her parents will be finding out in the morning. We have to do something. Now, right now! If we don't stop this . . . We have to. Now!"

"All right, let's get to work. Where was she last?"

"She's been doing concerts in New York City, I heard it on the news this morning. The abduction will happen at 11 P.M., 10 P.M, our time, tonight. She will be taken out of her room, sound asleep. She will not wake up. I see him crawling through a window. Just picking her up out of her bed and leaving through the door. We must go!"

"New York City? We've never projected there before. Is anyone familiar with New York?" Louis seemed daunted by a city this formidable.

"It's no different from any projection, Louis. There's no time and space, remember? If you are unsure of this trip, you don't have to do it."

"No, Professor. I'm in this with all of you. I will go."

"Good! Hurry!" Meredith was inspiration for our quick departure. As we all thought of Karen Slade, music permeated our reality. Her music, a gentle piano lightly playing in the background, growing in strength and volume as we approached the place from which she would be abducted. We worked to change the time period we were in. Finding her asleep, we knew we had been successful. Using all available energy, we changed our surroundings to the place she would be taken after her abduction.

"What is after this child? What is this place?" Alex's questions were inspired by our newly discovered surroundings. We were in some workshop, in a basement location. Figures stood realistically around the walls. But they were not breathing. "What are these?" "They're mannequins of some kind. Find a sign. Are we in a museum? They are mannequins all right, but they're mostly of children, little girls." Meredith said with a tone of disgust. This was a sickening, strange, eerie place, and discovering the mannequins made it even less comfortable.

"It's some sort of workshop. Mannequins from department stores or made for department stores." Mark struggled to explain.

"I don't think so, Mark. I think if Macy's needed a mannequin they would solicit one from a manufacturer, not some basement hobby enthusiast. This place is sinister." Meredith voiced all of our feelings. It was sinister. Music played softly as we searched the premises for its owner. Music. Someone was playing a piano. As we listened, we realized we were listening to a piece Meredith played frequently at the counseling center. It was Karen Slade's gifted version of Mozart's Piano Concerto No. 21 in C, "Elvira Madigan." The lilting tones, the sureness of delivery, contradicted the danger the child was in.

"Why would we come here? Is this some sort of bad horror movie?"

"No, Alex. That's Karen's recording. Whoever this is, he's obviously obsessed with Karen's talent, maybe with the child, as well." Meredith calmly concluded.

"What is that noise?" A sound as if a child were weeping started as a whisper, then grew to consume our surroundings. "Who's there?"

"Remain calm, Amy. This is no harmful entity. I know this energy. Mimma? Mimma, is that you? Please, Mimma, speak with us!"

The rest of the Angels looked at Meredith as though she had lost her mind.

"Mimma! Meredith, what would Mimma be doing here?" Alex inquired, obviously perplexed.

"I don't know, Alex. But she's here. She's here somewhere and she's scared." Meredith continued her plea. "Mimma, you are safe with us, you know that don't you? Please, show yourself."

The room seemed to shift with light. It illuminated in a fashion not known to science. A flash of a glow here, then there, then glowing from several directions at once and evolving, as though reaching us was some fantastic journey of light descending into physicality. Mimma made that journey with some stress. She appeared before us, still in her modest gown, as we had left her. And more frightened than when we had originally discovered her.

"Mimma! What has brought you to this terrible place, child?" Meredith rushed to the girl's side.

"It's my uncle! He's here and he is evil! The girl . . . the girl is in danger!" Mimma desperately formed her words through tears, all the time wringing her hands.

"How could your uncle be here, Mimma? We're in a different century for heaven's sake!" Alex chided the girl accusing her of wasting valuable time.

Meredith stood with her arm around Mimma. "Alex, please! Tell us, Mimma. Why do you think your uncle is here?"

"He is evil. He was born again, into your time. In this life his name is Collin Grant. All of my memories have returned since you helped to release me from that cabin. All of my memories . . ." The child was once again in tears.

I approached Mimma. "It's all right, Dear. We will help. Just tell us what you know."

"I know now why Uncle Jess had taken me to that cabin. He wanted no one to find me! He wanted me to die there alone! Because . . . because I knew!"

"Knew what, Mimma?" Meredith encouraged gently.

"I knew what he had done. Children, he loved little children. He would carve wood to look like little girls, and each time he carved a piece of wood, another child disappeared.

I followed him one night to the barn. I heard the child weeping in the barn! I waited until everyone slept, and I went to find her. She was tied up and I released her. When he awoke and found her gone, he was furious! He knew, since there was no change in Mother's or Grandfather's attitude toward him, that they had not discovered and released her. He knew it was me! Mother had asked him to go into town for her. Before I could go to them, he grabbed me and threw me in the wagon. My head hit something hard. No one knew he had taken me. When I woke up in the cabin, he beat me again. He left me in the cabin to die alone because he was afraid I would tell. And now, now he's here to harm children all over again. You must stop him! You can't let him do this!" Mimma sobbed once again.

"We will stop him, Mimma. You were very brave to come here to help. We are so grateful to you." Meredith consoled the childlike spirit.

"How, Meredith? How will we stop him?" Louis was determined to help, but was lost for ideas.

"Search this place. Besides the mannequins, there must be something else that would incriminate him. Look through everything. Leave no corner without a search." And we did as she suggested. "Mimma, you have done your job. Go. There is no reason for you to stay here. Karen will be all right. I promise."

Mimma put her arms around Meredith's neck to hug her good-bye, and she was gone.

We found many things that told of the twisted nature of Collin's being. Nothing was hidden since he expected no intrusion. We found photographs, letters, magazines, unimaginable collections of pornography. We were exhausting ourselves using energy to absorb the aura of materials scattered about the room. Obviously we couldn't move it, but we could sense it.

"I can't look at this stuff anymore. It's making me sick!" Amy needed a break.

I had found clippings of murdered children. All little girls. "It's all right, Amy. We have all we need. We have seen enough, let's go home."

Back in our safe counseling center, we opened our eyes simultaneously. We had to find help and find it now.

Mark woke up talking. "No one is going to believe us if we start making phone calls. What do we do?"

"We have to find someone who can communicate with us on a psychic level, Mark. Someone with the same ability we have. Preferably someone involved in the New York City Police Department. Meredith. Meredith? Meredith, talk to me!" I shook her gently but she didn't respond. Her eyes were wide open, but she seemed not to be with us. "Meredith for God's sake!"

Finally, she spoke. "I'm all right, Lang. Stop shaking me, you will bring me back to my body. I have to stay out." It was her voice, but it seemed to filter through her like a poor recording.

"Meredith, what have you done?"

"I'm not in my body, Lang. I am experiencing a duality. I am with you, but I'm here, as well."

"Here? Where is here?"

"The police station, New York City. I am following a detective in this office. He seems to be aware that someone or something is behind him. He keeps turning to look, but he sees nothing. I have to use more energy to help him to see me. I won't be able to speak for a few minutes. Let me do this, Lang. It's our only chance. Stop worrying!"

Even out of her body, this woman made a point of reading my mind! Her few minutes seemed like an eternity as we sat silently waiting for the life to come back to her eyes, or at least a word from her lips. "He sees me now! He's frightened. I have to calm him. Give me more time." And again, we lost her.

Five minutes passed and I could no longer do nothing. "Meredith? Meredith, can you hear me?"

Her body bolted forward, and she shook her head. "I'm all right, Lang. There's a stunned detective in New York City, though! I told him to guard Karen Slade and bring backup. I told him he would apprehend a serial murderer and save the child's life. I told him that once he was apprehended, a search of his residence would turn up enough evidence to put him away for the rest of his life. He thinks I'm his guardian angel. I had all I could do to keep him from falling to his knees! I intend to stay with him during this. You may all leave. This is my mission, now."

None of us left. We kept watch over Meredith's body as it peacefully slept without its normally animated spirit. We had no intention of leaving, in case Meredith should need us. Her account of the night's proceedings should interest you.

Detective Benton was remarkable. After he recovered from the shock of seeing a spirit, he went to find his partner, then summoned a selected group of officers. Some of them were at home and he called them. They met at New York's fashionable Waterford Hotel that evening. Daniel Benton kept me near him with tiny silent pleas for help. He would say, 'You got me into this, Angel, don't let me down now.'

I had no intention of letting him down. I was praying silently that he would not let Karen down. He was her only hope. The concierge cooperated with the officers and detectives in the lobby. They came undercover. After showing adequate identification, they explained that they had a tip on a possible kidnapping. The child in danger was Karen Slade. The concierge wanted none of this type of liability. "Whatever you have to do to protect her, you will have our full cooperation." He seemed grateful that the police were on top of the situation. It never occurred to him to ask how they knew of the impending danger.

A stakeout was their next step. I had informed Detective Benton of the time the kidnapping would take place. They would be ready and waiting. Dressed in casual clothes, they were given a suite on the same floor occupied by Karen Slade. They spent more time lurking in the hallways and hiding in the staircells than they did in their suite of rooms.

My attention was drawn away from the officers to the side of this criminal, Collin Grant. I watched Collin Grant on his way to the hotel. He was dressed in black to blend with the night. He looked from one side to the other, keeping track of who might be watching him. The only one paying attention to what he was doing was me, the one he couldn't see.

As he entered the hotel lobby, he walked to the desk and spoke to an employee of the hotel. When that person walked away, Collin turned the computer monitor and scanned it briefly, skillfully, and without emotion. He then headed for the elevator.

As he stepped out into the hallway, two pairs of eyes watched him. Detective Benton was alerted. "That's him." I said quietly in his ear. "Don't let him near that child."

"Oh, don't worry!" Officer Benton responded to me, unaware that his partner was listening to his one-sided conversation.

"Did you say something, Dan?"

"Uh, no, Bill. I was clearing my throat."

From Bill's expression, I knew he didn't quite buy that explanation. But my goal was to protect this child at any cost. "Watch him carefully. He is cunning," I admonished. "He will find an unobserved entry" This time, rather than risk his partner's mental evaluation of him, Dan Benton just nodded his head. But he couldn't help but ask, "Stay with me, Angel."

"What?"

"Nothing, Bill. I was talking to myself."

"Well stop it! You're spooking me!"

I gave Dan as much information as I could. "This suite has an adjoining room. That's where he will get in. First through a lobby window overlooking the courtyard, then forcing the interconnecting door. Then it's only a matter of finding the correct bedroom and entering through the door. Hurry, Dan. He's slipping into Karen's room. He's there now! Now, Dan! Hurry!"

The door to the suite was skillfully broken into. This was no time for hesitation. The 'Angel' whispering in Dan's ear was becoming increasingly agitated! They did not have a moment to spare. Aside from his ghoulish activity, the kidnapper had an uncanny ability to slip in and out of places unnoticed. His movement was catlike, and he was equally quiet. Dan entered through the courtyard window of the child's darkened room and stopped him, with Karen in his arms, on his way back through the door. One handcuff linked their wrists while Bill jerked the sleeping child from her kidnapper's arms.

Hearing the commotion, Karen's nanny bolted from her room. "What are you doing? Put that child down!"

She was shown identification from an officer, and Karen was handed to her. Clutching the child close, she sat and watched as they led Collin Grant away, ultimately to a place where he would never again harm another child.

"Good work, Mimma. We would not have done this as easily without all your help." Meredith, returning from her adventure spoke to Mimma as she slowly returned to consciousness. Light and mist surrounded us at the counseling center in our drawing room. It was Mimma descending into our world for a visit.

"Yes, Mimma. You have done well," I said as she took form before our eyes.

"The little girl is safe now?"

"Yes, Mimma, Karen is safe."

"He won't be able to hurt anyone again, will he?"

"No, Mimma. He was stopped because of you. We finally have a real angel to help us!"

Mimma found her mission through our own. We see her often as she finds missing children and leads us simultaneously to assist them. There are many on the other side who work for the children's benefit. And the children of this world have a true guardian angel in Mimma as she darts between worlds. We are so proud of her. Karen Slade and her special talent brings Mimma to our side regularly to visit. The sound of her music entices her into our world and she lends her energy to the group as we meditate and project to find our missing children.

That is my story. As you have read this book, I feel you all have become my students. And so I must give you an assignment!

Learn of your true nature. Understand that you are one with the universe, one with all who surround you, one with all life. Take comfort in your place, for you are a cherished soul and one that we could not do without. Learn to understand how, to the greatest extent, you control your own environment. Explore your nature. Learn to ask for help in your lessons. Nothing you ask will ever go unanswered because you are so very important. But you must learn to anticipate the answer and "hear" it when it is offered. Look for happiness and surround yourself with the beauty this world has to offer. Take care of each other and maintain each other's joy.

As a resident of this wonderful planet Earth, help to make it one of the billions of life-affirming consistent planets in all of the universes. That is its destiny, and it's waiting for our help to lead it and to realize its destiny. Once realized, all of nature and spirit will coexist in complete harmony.

And my final wish to you as I conclude my story: May the Angels always be nearby for your children.